CW01501921

COLONEL BRANDON'S WIDOW AND WILLOUGHBY

A Sense and Sensibility Variation Sequel
Copyright © 2019 by Marianna Green

All rights reserved. Except for use in any review, the reproduction or utilization of this work in whole or in part in any form by any electronic, mechanical or other means, now known or hereinafter invented, including xerography, photocopying and recording, or in any information storage or retrieval system, is forbidden without the written permission of the publisher.

This is a work of fiction. Names, characters, places and incidents are either the product of the author's imagination or are used fictitiously, and any resemblance to actual persons, living or dead, business establishments, events or locales is entirely coincidental.

Printed in the USA.

Cover Design and Interior Format

Colonel Brandon's
Widow &
Willoughby

A REGENCY NOVEL

MARIANNA GREEN

To Harriet Lark
With many thanks for her invaluable help.

CHAPTER ONE

"DID YOU KNOW, MRS. BRANDON, that Mr. Willoughby and his wife were back in Town, but left early for separate locations? They had everyone talking of their indecorous behaviour again. They say that she slapped him across the face in their curricle." Miss Steele giggled.

Colonel Brandon's widow received this piece of gossip from Town with indifference, while her sister Elinor turned in indignation. Contrary to the common – and erroneous – view of the compensations of aging, the years had not brought Miss Steele any advance in sense. This remark was certainly made through tactlessness rather than the malice that would have inspired it from her sister. Still, it was in poor taste.

"There is no need to repeat such things, Miss Steele." Elinor kept her tone mild.

Marianne murmured something, and continued to stare out of the window at the view of the lush park of Delaford, which sloped down to the ha-ha that divided it from the meadows where cattle lay down in the heat of the day.

She was aware that Elinor was concerned about her being unable to throw off her melancholy. Her sister had always believed that one had a social duty to hide personal feelings behind an air of composure. She understood how Colonel Brandon's death from a sudden illness at the age of forty was a loss which his wife of four years must feel profoundly; still, Marianne knew that for Elinor, her mourning had in it something excessive.

Marianne had always been eager in all emotions, quick alike in approval and disgust, joy and sorrow. In recent years, and especially since her marriage to the Colonel, she had tried to control this; nevertheless, it remained a submerged but strong part of her nature. Her happiness with Colonel Brandon had perhaps only been exceeded by her former anguish at Willoughby's betrayal of her to marry an heiress.

Now, on Elinor's rebuke, Miss Steele laughed again. "Lud, I am forever saying the wrong thing, Mrs. Ferrrs. As it has been a year now since the poor dear Colonel's passing, I sought to distract Mrs. Brandon with some news from Town. "

"It was eleven months last Friday," Marianne said flatly. She knew she should not have spoken, but resented anyone being vague about the length of time since the Colonel's death.

Miss Steele, apparently not hearing, laughed. "They say that Mrs. Willoughby often takes too much wine; has become quite the toper indeed. 'Tis too true her face shows it."

"Really, Miss Steele —" Elinor began again.

"Do not blame me for starting the rumour. I had it from our friend Widow Jennings, who is always in the know. They say that Mrs. Willoughby drinks because he neglects her shamelessly, and that makes him even colder to her, especially as it so ruins her complexion, which was ever sallow. Well, all know that he takes too much himself, but it doesn't show on him. Widow Jennings did say that when they were last over at Allenham, poor Mrs. Willoughby was hardly fit to be seen in the morning… No more of that, you frown so on me – though my sister Lucy says it is Mrs. Willoughby's own fault for not knowing how to handle him."

Elinor cut in, "How is Lucy? I recollect you have seen her since last she visited us."

Miss Steeele was happy enough to turn the conversation to her younger sister.

Elinor said, "Indeed?" and "How charming," about the new barouche, while Marianne stared unheeding out of the window. It was like the days of their girlhood; when Elinor had always been the one to practice the social graces.

Marianne knew that Elinor had turned the conversation out of disgust at its vulgarity, not through fear that talk of Willoughby and his wife might distress her. It had been many years since Marianne's feelings had been hurt through hearing of the Willoughbys.

In the early days of her marriage to Colonel Brandon, Marianne had been uneasy at the mention of his name. But then, as she had come to love Brandon in a way that she would have found incredible a couple of years before, thoughts of Willoughby ceased to be painful to her, save that she was sorry to hear that he had drifted further into debauchery.

Before their marriage, Marianne had forgiven
Colonel Brandon for being in his late thirties, no
brilliant conversationalist, and for not playing and
singing. She had even overlooked his wearing a
flannel waistcoat on a damp, raw day – a huge con-
cession.

Afterwards, she had come to treasure his excel-
lence of mind and temper, and this had led to her
seeing in him an allure which she would once
have believed impossible. Yet, she had not loved
him with the infatuated and guileless passion with
which she had doted on the handsome, dashing
and finally unprincipled Willoughby.

Now, for the first time in years, she found herself brooding about Willoughby. Wishing to turn
her thoughts, she broke into Miss Steele's raptures
about that new barouche of her sister's to exclaim,
"It is so oppressively warm today: I wonder if we
might take a stroll in the garden under the cover
of our parasols."

"Indeed, you must be monstrous hot in that
black bombazine," said Miss Steele. "Even with a
parasol, we risk giving ourselves freckles. I always
say I am past the time of life when the state of
my complexion need concern me. 'La,' I say to my
cousins, 'If a certain gentleman who shall remain
nameless mistook me for the younger sister, it is
all one to me at my age; I am past the time of life
for beaux.'"

The Marianne of seven years ago would have
ignored this plea for a compliment; this, not – as
now – because she was too distracted to react to it,
but because would have she thought it unworthy
of notice. The Marianne of later years would have

said kindly, as Elinor now did, "That is a compliment, your sister looking so youthful."

Elinor and Marianne both acknowledged that the former Lucy Steele had kept her youthful looks; both put this down to her having no conscience – a far better way of preserving a youthful complexion than *Ninon de L'enclos*.

Miss Steele glowed. "That is what my cousins say. I don't think I will join you in a walk, if Mrs. Brandon will excuse me. Heyday, I am all admiration of your grounds, but I will go back to the parsonage to rest before dinner. It is never dull at your house, with the children so full of spirits; it puts me in mind of Lady Middleton's darlings, when Lucy and I visited as girls."

Elinor was shocked. "I hope not, indeed. Should they ever behave so, I beg you to tell Mr. Ferrars or myself, and we will see to their correction at once."

Out in the pleasure gardens, the two sisters walked slowly towards the herb garden which had always been Marianne's favourite spot. Elinor, glancing at Marianne's face, engaging even when sad and pale, said, "I am sorry for my guest's thoughtless chatter. It must be trying to you. But I felt, as she was eager to call in on us, and could break her journey on the way, it was only fair to invite her to stay some couple of days. She is after all, an old acquaintance."

"It does not trouble me at all, truly. But Elinor, the workings of providence are sometimes so sad. I have lost my Colonel, and while I came to value him as he deserved, I remember how little I did at the first, when I wasted months pining over Willoughby. – And poor Mrs. Willoughby! I can't avoid hearing how things are between them. Everybody must, it is so talked about."

Elinor shook her head. "She is greatly to be pitied: − as much for the misguided wilfulness that
led her to fix on a man who could not return
her feelings, as for his treatment of her and her
own abandonment of self- respect in creating such
scenes. It is sad that with so many superior quali-
ties, he should make a choice that has brought out
the worst in him."

She frowned as she went on, "But then, self-re-
straint was never a characteristic of *his,* any more
than resignation to his indifference seems to have
been one of *hers.* Therefore, I am sorry to say that
they are entirely suited as a source of torment to
each other."

Marianne bit her lip. "It is difficult at times to
reconcile what we see in life with a benign providence, and that is setting aside that we come from
the part of society where our sorrows are at least
not through want…I hope I don't shock you,
Elinor; even the Colonel − orthodoxy itself on
religious matters − said such things now and then."

Elinor took her hand. "Edward always says that
we must trust to such questions being beyond
human understanding, my dear, and strain our
finite minds no further."

Marianne knew that her tendency to brood on
such matters was encouraged by her marriage with
Colonel Brandon having proved childless, unlike
that of Edward and Elinor, who had an addition to
their family every couple of years.

If she had been as busy as Elinor as the wife of a
hard working clergyman and mother of a growing
family on an income that was only adequate (and

it was lucky that Edward now had a better living than the one on which he and Elinor had started married life), she would have had no time to brood on such things. Even during her happy years with the Colonel, she had tended to do so. The blunt Edward told her that she had a morbid streak.

Elinor continued, "But what we must not trust to, is our fellow creatures' good sense. Willoughby and his wife went into their unhappy union with their eyes open and have ever since made the worst of it. The responsibility for that rests entirely with themselves."

She added with a smile, "I know that your own loss makes you not — as is too often the case — oblivious to the suffering of others, but rather, inclined to feel them more. Still, you must not be encouraged to indulge your tendency to take things to extremes."

Marianne had to smile in return, and they fell silent for a few moments. They wandered on in the heat, pausing to watch a heap of stones, piled by the gardener for use in the rockery, covered in basking tortoiseshell butterflies hatched by the weather unusually hot for spring.

The sisters avoided speaking of what their old friend Mrs. Jennings soon suggested, when she had called on them fresh from Town a couple of weeks since: that Marianne's new widowed status had stoked the fires of the Willoughby's marital difficulties, which sometimes smouldered, and sometimes blazed.

Suddenly, Marianne spoke out. "On the question of making the worst of the situations in which we find ourselves: it is more than time for me to exert myself. I must not distress my relatives and weaken my health through indulging sorrow over my loss of the Colonel too long, as I once did over the loss of the far less worthy Willoughby. That betrayal was, after all, my gain. In a month it will be time to go into half mourning. I must see about having a couple of lilac dresses made up."

Elinor took her hand and squeezed it. "What best, do you think, would raise your spirits?"

"I want to visit Barton Cottage, and enjoy our mother's company and Margaret's, before she is married. I will go on some of our old rambles in the area. – And of course, I must call at Barton Park and see our old friends there," she added with all the stoicism that she could muster. Then, she went on to true heroism by adding, "If it would be convenient for you for Miss Steele to prolong her visit by another day or so, I could take her with me in my carriage to Exeter."

CHAPTER TWO

MARIANNE STILL NO SOONER HAD an idea than she was eager to act on it. She set off within two days, with one manservant, luggage, and Miss Steele's talk. Elinor only hoped that it would not be about topics likely to increase her sister's melancholy.

But, as ever, Marianne, when determined on a course of action could be relied upon to follow it to completion, and she was now resolved to recover her spirits.

She had even resolved to take a lesson by the widow Jennings joviality, if not her vulgarity. She knew Mrs. Jennings would be visiting her elder daughter and son-in-law at Barton Park and hoped to gain from her example of cheerfulness.

A widow of fifteen years, Mrs. Jennings' chief wish was to make all her acquaintance happy. This she strove to do by marrying them off to each other, and she was disappointed that her schemes for Miss Steele had so far come to nothing.

Value Colonel Brandon though she had, Mrs. Jennings must feel a little cheated that, after all her efforts to promote his marriage to Marianne, he had so far forgotten himself as to survive it by only five years, and to leave his widow childless.

Marianne could only hope that as she had not yet been a widow twelve months, even Mrs. Jennings would not try to remarry her yet. Still, she had no doubt that she would begin soon enough.

For her own part, she was determined to stay a widow for the rest of her life. The comfortable settlement that Colonel Brandon had left her must attract some suitors. Marianne, no longer a sheltered girl of seventeen, realised that, and she was determined to keep such men at arms' length.

The estate of Delaford was entailed to the next male heir. This youth was not of age, and his guardians had shown none of the haste to gain possession that Marianne's brother had shown on their father's death. In fact, the guardian had written to Marianne, urging her to feel under no pressure to move.

At that time, Marianne had been too stunned by grief to exert herself in any way. But now, aware that she must think in terms of making her home elsewhere, she had decided to move back in with her mother over at Barton in Devonshire.

Mrs. Dashwood still lived with her youngest daughter on restricted means in Barton Cottage, and Marianne hoped that adding her own income to the household would increase their comforts.

On the journey between Delaford and Barton Marianne needed all the patience she had learned in her years with the Colonel. Miss Steele's talk was incessant and insipid:

"La, Mrs. Brandon, take a peek at that curricle. Sure, it is something on the lines of Lucy's. – she and Robert had such a fight over the hangings you can't think; but he would have his way, though she declared the end result dismal. – Lud, there's a leveret, near ran under our wheels! – I am so glad that we aren't likely to be held up by highwaymen as in the days of our parents and grandparents, but it would have been romantic, don't you think, to come on a fine beau who gave you a dance? – Only look, there's an inn called *The Kings Head!* I declare, my cousins still tease me whenever we pass an inn of that name, and bid me beware, for it was in *The King's Head* near Highgate that I was sorely vexed by a very smart young beau, who would pester me with compliments. – La, if we are not at the posting inn already."

But Marianne when determined could surmount any difficulty; she survived many hours of such chatter, arriving at Barton Cottage and her mother and Margaret's arms with her wits intact, if fatigued.

As when Mrs. Dashwood had been at Delaford before, Marianne and her mother found comfort in uniting their sadness over Colonel Brandon's death.

Marianne's younger sister Margaret joined them in this whenever she could depress her spirits enough to match their mood. But though she had liked her brother-in-law, and felt for Marianne's loss, she could not be unhappy for long at a time. She was recently engaged to an eligible young man to whom she had a strong attachment, and could think of little but her wedding.

Though her sisters had tried over the years to persuade her out of her own version of the sensibility which Marianne had herself once eagerly cultivated – with Marianne using her own disappointment as an object lesson – their efforts had not been successful.

Now Margaret was as happy in this springtime of her feelings as Marianne had once been in hers. As a fond sister, Marianne could not say a word to detract from that. Margaret's lover called whenever he could; when he was kept away, he wrote. Then she dashed from the room with his letter in her hand, to come back ten minutes later and sit shivering and blushing and unable to speak coherently on any subject for the next half hour.

Margaret secretly hoped that her favourite sister would come in time to a second union where she had the passionate love which Margaret suspected had been lacking in that solid, but unexciting, union with the excellent Colonel. Margaret herself had never been at ease with him, as she was with Edward, and had once been with the disgraced Willoughby. She had always felt that one had to be on one's best behaviour to live up to the Colonel's elevated ideas. No wonder Marianne had become so serious.

Secretly, Margaret found it hard not to think it inconsiderate of the Colonel to die before her wedding, so that it had to be deferred. Of course, she showed nothing of this. She was no longer the gauche child who had joined Mrs. Jennings in teasing Elinor about the secret admirer whose name began with an 'F'.

Mrs. Dashwood, for her part, was not a woman given over to self analysis. Otherwise, she might have noticed that in her mourning for Colonel Brandon, a sense of guilt played some part in her mainly genuine sorrow. She could not forget that she had not at first seen the Colonel as an attractive prospect for Marianne, and that she had come to recognise his worth long after Elinor.

Thus, mother and daughter mourned together. Still, Marianne had vowed to exert herself, and she did. She went on with the studies which she had taken up at seventeen, and had later thought to abandon with the birth of her first child. As she and the Colonel had remained childless, she had continued with them ever since, and advanced far in history, Latin and modern languages. In Colonel Brandon she had lost a fine tutor; she would continue nevertheless.

She was working on making up a wardrobe of half mourning for herself, and also on Margaret's wedding clothes. Though as a girl she had hated cards, she even played *vingt-et-un* and cribbage with Mrs. Dashwood and Margaret —and Margaret's betrothed, if he happened to be visiting. As ever, she played and sang of an evening.

They were a family group, as Sir John and Lady Middleton were away from Barton Park for some weeks, and would be returning with Mrs. Jennings. The years had made Sir John no less sociable, and he was still as eager to surround himself with lively people – especially young ones – and to think up entertainments for them.

Marianne, as a widow still in mourning, would

not at once be expected to attend balls, dinners and outings even when her twelvemonth was up. But no doubt she would be invited over to take tea with them and for other family gatherings. She vowed to endure the disruptive children with stoicism and to play every song that the family requested, however foolish.

During this period alone with her mother and sister, she sighed sometimes as she watched Margaret and her lover. Yet, if she found excuses to leave the room and the lovers alone together, it was not because she was on the brink of tears, but through tact.

Carrying out her resolve, two days after the period of deep mourning had ended, Marianne put on a new half mourning gown. As lilac had always suited her well, her new outfits were becoming, particularly as, with all the walking she had been doing with Margaret, she had got back much of the bloom to her cheeks.

One day, Marianne found herself preceding Margaret along a path that led into Allenham Valley, and passed by a farm. From here, the roofs of Allenham House, over a mile away, were visible. Marianne had once seen the inside of this house, in circumstances that she preferred not to remember. From here, a short walk led back to a particular hill overlooking Barton Cottage, where Marianne had once sprained her ankle and been rescued by a dashing young man.

On this day, as the sisters came up to the farm, an infant toddled out of the back door and made, as if following a plan he had determined on, straight for the uncovered well at the end of the vegetable plot. He pulled himself up to the brink through determination alone, and was standing on the edge, babbling to himself, as Marianne and Margaret came in sight of the garden.

Marianne pulled up her skirts and dashed towards the well. Margaret, younger but less agile, was at first close in pursuit, but soon fell behind. Even as they ran, the infant slipped and sat down. Now, with both legs dangling over the brink, he began to scream. This alerted a rider who was coming down the track from Allenham House from the other side.

The rider urged his horse into a gallop. Even as he did, Marianne had vaulted the wall in a flurry of petticoats to gain the well. Now the child stood up, swayed, and toppled over the brink.

She caught him, stopping his fall. But in throwing herself across the parapet, she forced much of the breath from her lungs by falling against the wall herself. It took all her strength to hold onto the infant. She had none to spare to pull him any further out of danger; she could only gasp for air, long for Margaret's arrival, and dread that her fingers might give way.

But before her sister came up, she heard hoof beats, and then running feet, and moments later, male hands relieved her of her hold on her wailing burden.

"Now then, youngster, you'll be well enough; run in to Mama, and let me see to the lady," said a well-remembered voice, and Marianne could neither rise, nor speak, nor prevent the man from lifting her up, as he once had before.

CHAPTER THREE

MARGARET HURRIED UP. RECOGNIS-ING WILLOUGHBY, she was lost for words. Unlike her older sisters, she had never yet had to use the forms of politeness when meeting him in society. Tactless as she knew it would be to leave these two once sweethearts together, she felt her presence to be awkward for them both. She took up the child, and stood indecisive.

"I don't think your sister is much hurt, Miss Margaret," said Willoughby. "Miss Margaret, do please step up to the door to ask the woman to bring out a glass of wine, or some such thing."

Margaret went gladly enough with the infant towards the back door.

Marianne now had some of her breath back. "Thank you…Sir…" she said breathlessly. "You may let me go, now." Her voice was scarcely understandable for breathlessness, and she could hardly blame him for not responding to it as he began to carry her across the garden.

She saw her situation was ridiculous, and thought any attempt at dignified rebuke must make it still more so. She was shocked to find herself once more in this man's arms, as she had longed to be for so long until Colonel Brandon had claimed her. Though too startled to feel any sensation from a touch that had once made her tingle, she longed to escape his embrace. She began to gasp out her request again.

He seemed not to hear, purposely, she suspected. He went on striding over with her towards a rough wooden bench. Even when he reached it, he did not put her down.

Instead he stood, gazing down at her. "It's been so long, and every day has been torment," he said. "I know I should commiserate with you on his loss, but – forgive me – all I can think of is that at last I hold you in my arms again."

The bright eyes looking down at her seemed unchanged. They had not become red and puffy from excess, though she had heard that both Mr. Willoughby and his wife took too much strong liquor too often. There were, however, lines about those eyes and his lips that she guessed came less from the years – he would now be in his early thirties, after all – than debauchery.

That hard living was written in everything about him, from a certain wildness at the back of his eyes, to a greater recklessness in his manner. But he was still as handsome as ever; his hair as thick and wavy, and full of chestnut gleams, his features as straight and strong, and his lips as firm as before.

As she made to free herself of his hold, he set her down on the bench. "There's no need to fear, I shan't try and carry you off, like to some dastardly villain in one of those plays we used to laugh over. Yet, probably I am that dastardly villain in your eyes forever; it is the least that I deserve. Still, you have hurt yourself, and you need to rest and recover your strength. It is fitting that we should meet again in such dramatic circumstances, and you saved that adventurer's life: even on my horse, I was not in time."

The strength returning to her limbs with every breath, Marianne could now resist actively. "For shame, Mr. Willoughby, to speak so to me. I am appalled at you, a married man, addressing such words to me, particularly when I have only lately been widowed."

Far from looking rebuked, he said, "Humph!" From the look in his eyes, she felt she had reason to be thankful that he said no more.

Marianne's ribs ached and her limbs felt weak, but she rose to the occasion. "I repeat I am appalled at you, Sir. How dare you speak such words to me? Whatever would my dear Colonel have made of such conduct?"

He turned his head away to mutter something that included words that sounded remarkably like, 'The Devil' but as he had spoken under his breath, she was glad to be able to ignore this.

He controlled himself, and turned about again. "Forgive me, Mrs. Brandon. I was shocked into being too open in my protestations of regard. But you know – you cannot fail to know – what they have always been. When I saw you collapsed by that well, all my glib society demeanour fell away as some mask. That was just as when I heard once that you were dying of a fever and I rode like the devil to beg your forgiveness. Then, I cared not a jot if I acted like a character from some romance or no."

Marianne could not but be moved, however shocking his conduct. She could not entirely blame him for his the violence of his expressions. For reasons that were unclear to her, this was the more true as she remembered a superstitious action she had taken once, years ago, at this same well, before her marriage, and before she came to value Colonel Brandon. However, she had no intention of telling him about that.

She said instead, "Please try to calm yourself, Mr. Willoughby. You speak of the past; what you then said to my sister that day was wrong. It is doubly so, now; nay, more. – How can you imagine, apart from the duty you owe to your wife, that I can hear such words when my own husband has only been lost to me a year? – Your words are not only an insult to your own wife, but one to the sincerity of my own regard for the Colonel. "

He dropped his eyes. She was forced to marvel, as she had so often when he was paying court to her, at the length and thickness of his lashes. He gazed hard at his boots for a moment, the colour rising in his face, and then that seemingly frank gaze met her own. "I must seem like an unfeeling brute, I know. I mean no insult to the strength of your attachment to the Colonel. He was a far better man than me, though that would be easy enough. Believe me, if I thought I had a chance of being alone with you to say what I must on some other occasion, I would not think of imposing on you now. Still, I know that I have not. You will avoid me assiduously, and given my former, to say the least, ungallant – not to say despicable – treatment of you, I can scarcely blame you."

She could think of no immediate reply, and he hurried on, "And so, the then Miss Elinor did pass those words of mine on to you? Ah! I feared she disapproved of them too much. She advised me to try and make the best life with my wife. You might as well advise a man whose idiocy has sent him to hell to make the best of it."

He regarded Marianne now, with all the old admiration he had once lavished on her at their meetings. This he had often turned on her when they were forced to meet at social occasions, and he thought himself unobserved.

Of course, he had been observed – particularly by Mrs. Willoughby – whose fortune, rich dress, becoming headdresses, and fine jewellery could not make one iota less plain. Marianne pitied her.

"My sister gave you good advice then, Mr. Willoughby –" she began, but he was not attending.

He said, "Here's the goodwife now, all anxiety, and I see Miss Margaret has had the presence of mind to ask her for some elderberry wine. I fear it will be nothing more palatable."

The farmer's wife was full of apologies for the mischief that her infant had brought about, and overwhelmed with gratitude for his rescue. She was shocked that the young widow had fallen down and bruised herself, and in a tizzy less she should be taken with a type of genteel fit. Her nervousness made the West Country turn to her speech far stronger. At times they were hard put to make out what she said.

She was the more anxious, as she recognised Mr.

Willoughby as Mrs. Smith's heir and the future squire. She begged them to enter her parlour, and apologised for its condition.

"Don't trouble yourself about that, Mistress. But that well needs covering," said Willoughby.

Marianne did what she could to reassure her that would be unnecessary; she had only a couple of slight bruises and she and Margaret would soon be on their way. She assured the woman that her elderberry wine was delicious. She only hoped that the woman missed Willoughby's grimace as he tasted his own portion, and the sleight of hand by which he poured it away.

Willoughby looked thoughtful. "I think you are too shaken to walk home, even if you would do me the honour of leaning on my arm the whole way, which I think you will not. I could ride back to Allenham and get out the carriage, of course."

"Nonsense!" Marianne spoke with the curtness that she had avoided for years in her wish to escape from him. "I would not dream of putting Mrs. Smith to such inconvenience."

She stood up, but to her annoyance, she swayed, and had to lean on Margaret's arm. Willoughby's hands reached out for her, seemingly without his volition.

The farmer's wife wrung her own hands. "Ah, Ma'am, you be unfit to take a step, and we have nothing to offer you but that sad cart. 'Tis unsuited for gentry and oft loaded with mangle worzels."

"I think it may do for us this once, with a dusting down, eh, Mrs. Brandon?" said Mr. Willoughby. "It is very good of you. I'll leave my own horse here, and drive the ladies back." He glanced out at the meadow where the horse was grazing. "It's a won-der he hasn't made for home; he's a wilful brute normally. He must have felt like some dinner."

From Margaret's look at these words, Marianne suspected that the horse was not the only hun-gry being among them. Determined to be free of Willoughby's presence, she urged the farmer's wife, "If your horse is placid enough, I am sure I may manage the cart."

"He's as placid as may be, Ma'am, but for a lady to be a-sitting in that thing…"

It took some effort to convince her, but even this availed Marianne nothing, for Willoughby would not be talked out of escorting them home, riding by the side of the trundling farm cart.

Mrs Dashwood was speechless at both the mode of their return, and to see Willoughby. Unlike that other occasion when he had come to her daugh-ter's rescue, she did not invite him in. She greeted him coolly. He did not linger beyond making his bow and outlining the details of the accident.

As he rode off in a flurry of dust up the summer lane, with his horse living up to the reputation he had given it by tossing its head and bucking slightly, she said, "Really, wretched man! Why must he impose himself upon us? He must be aware how unwelcome he is here. "

She glanced at Margaret, whom she was still in the habit of treating more or less as a child. Reflecting that she was of an age to hear such things, engaged as she now was, went on, "Was he intoxicated?"

Marianne had to smile. "Really, Mama, it was fortunate that he appeared when he did, or the baby might have fallen into the well. As for being intoxicated, he showed no sign of it."

Her mother stared. "It is magnanimous of you to be so warm in his justification, my dear, considering how little reason you have to defend his character."

"It used to be my fault to judge people harshly. It is one I try and avoid these days." Marianne spoke calmly enough, but something in her mother's gaze, both quizzing and anxious, made her blush.

She also found herself longing to be by herself, so that she could think about this meeting, both dramatic and absurd as it had been. She wanted to try and ascertain exactly what she felt about Willoughby's shocking and passionate words, which she now tried to believe might well have been caused by taking too much drink.

Fearing that this wish to brood about the adventure alone might be due to residual improper feelings for him, Marianne punished herself by keeping in her mother and sister's company until bedtime.

Mrs. Dashwood wished to discuss the meeting, if only for reassurance that her daughter's defence of Willoughby was only out of charity.

Marianne would have liked to reassure her. Still, she had always had difficulty in saying more than she felt. She had no wish to talk about Willoughby at the moment, being torn by stronger and more conflicting emotions about him than she had felt in years. Indignation at his actions and speeches warred with sympathy for his unhappiness.

She reminded herself that he had nobody to blame for that unhappiness but himself. He had married his wife for her money, sacrificing his own feelings and those of Marianne herself, and causing the unhappy woman who had set her heart on him at all costs a life of resentment.

It was probably only in human nature that he should regret this match even as he worked to bring it about. Certainly, everything that had come to Marianne's reluctant hearing over the past years confirmed that he had never ceased to regret her.

This had not precluded his engaging in pleasures of a wild, reckless kind. Still, his domestic life was as joyless as he had confided to Elinor on that day when, forgetting his pose of cynical indifference to Marianne, he had ridden in frantic haste to hear if she was dying, and if she could forgive him.

The union of the Willoughby's only resembled that of the Brandons in being childless. Unlike the latter couple, they had no common interests to compensate, unless an unfortunate tendency to over indulge in wine and other stimulants could count as a mutual source of diversion.

It is true that they did share in common a manner of relating to each other that involved raised voices behind slammed doors, angry silences and periods of cold civility; but this shared inclination brought them no closer together.

It could be further urged on their behalf, that in this conduct, they provided society with the diversion of much talk, and their staff with constant entertainment. Willoughby's confidential

valet knew all about his improper pursuits, while
his wife's lady's maid could recount how Mrs. Willoughby had cursed him for a fortune hunting
libertine in full hearing of the servants, and of how
savagely he had kicked shut her sitting room door
before retorting that, 'Devil take it, in his whole
worthless life, he had only cared for the former
Marianne Dashwood, and he would be damned if
he pretended anything else to please a scolding...'

But the reader does not wish to hear any more of
this vulgar dispute.

Seemingly their staff lacked any discretion. Soon
enough, the content of the Willoughbys' exchanges
leaked out into polite society, which showed still
less decorum in repeating them assiduously.

Many a man had dined out for a month on his
knowledge of episodes that ought to have been
cloaked in decent silence, and Miss Steele was one
of many maiden ladies agog for the latest outrage.

While Colonel Brandon had been alive his wife
had never regretted that decision of Willoughby's
as regards herself, feeling that it had saved her from
the degradation of a union with a libertine. But
now, doubts crept into her mind. Her thoughts
reached out to areas where she knew they should
not.

She rebuked herself again and again.

She suspected that the cause was the emptiness
of her life now that the Colonel had gone, and she
was no longer mistress of so delightful a house as
Delaford.

The Colonel had been a generous landlord to
his tenants, though not an extravagant one. He
and Marianne had led a quiet lifestyle when in the

countryside, though one that had involved visits to Town during the season, and driving out in a stylish carriage enough to satisfy any lingering pride of Marianne's.

Accordingly, Colonel Brandon had been able, even with so unexpected a fatal illness, to leave her a portion ample enough for her to live independently, if quietly, for the rest of her life. This is what she intended to do.

Being childless, she must find some other interest to occupy her. Certainly, she had no urge to follow the example of such widows as Mrs. Jennings, and make plans to marry off all of her younger acquaintance, while teasing every unattached male and female between the ages of fifteen and fifty about supposed attachments, however improbable.

Of course, Marianne would keep on with her studies. Still, as she had worked on them for a total of seven years now, this lacked the stimulus of novelty.

Her meeting with Willoughby had brought home to her the danger of having leisure hours with nothing absorbing to fill them. She saw that she must find one. When, therefore, she was quiet the evening after that encounter, her thoughts were on this as much as on Willoughby.

Mrs. Dashwood had, of course, no way of knowing this, and feared the worst. She had never been able either to stop loving Willoughby herself, and so her grudge against him was unforgiven.

After all, all of the family had been more or less in love with him. This was so of all the world save for moralists. He was one of those people on whom nature lavishes gifts, and who, instead of being grateful for such bounty, throw them away with abandon. He had squandered his charm and his talents, ruined Colonel Brandon's trusting ward Eliza, indulged in excesses, and brought unhappiness on himself and others.

Yet despite this, it was impossible to speak to him for two minutes without falling slightly under his spell, however uncharitably one might think on him when away from him. A man without his charm of glance and manner would possibly have become a social outcast had he behaved so, despite the advantage of a wife's fortune of fifty thousand pounds. Somehow, Willoughby was always forgiven.

He was even forgiven repeatedly by Mrs. Willoughby herself. She had after all sworn to love him till death, though her confidential maid knew that she kept an account of his infidelities in a little notebook, and also the shocking names he called her in temper, which the girl said 'must fair have scorched the paper.' So things had been going on for the last seven years, and looked to continue indefinitely.

Now, as the twilight descended on the valleys of Barton and Allenham, and the evensong of the birds drew to a close with the last of the pink fading from the sky, and Mrs. Dashwood rang for lights, she had vague and uneasy fears for Marianne that made her as unusually silent as her daughter.

Fortunately, Margaret's chatter made a diversion while they sat sewing and trying to soothe their ruffled feelings: -

"So, Marianne, your music's arrived. I am glad, as there is that song by Beethoven come, that Stephen likes so. You must try to help me learn to play it as well as you, though I can never have such ease on the keyboard…Ma'am, do you work upon the embroidery on the bodice of my new gown? I am so happy you undertake it, for while the girl deals well enough with the simpler designs, this must take all your skill… I do not wish to plague you, but do you think it might be ready by the family's return to Barton Park? Sir John has such diversions up his sleeve, you can't think. We are to visit all the local beauty sports, and perhaps even to go as far as the coast if the weather holds…Aren't you looking forward to it, Marianne? Oh, forgive me: that was thoughtless in me, I am so sorry!"

Marianne reassured her younger sister about that. In this she equivocated. Colonel Brandon had enjoyed taking part in all Sir John's entertainments except the one pleasure trip he had been forced to disrupt through having news of his young ward's desperate situation after her seduction by Willoughby. Any outing with Sir John brought back memories of the ones she had enjoyed with the Colonel.

Not wishing to dwell on this, she said instead, "Sir John's return to the neighbourhood must delight any person with that unquenchable passion for standing up at balls that goes with youth. Shall we see what we can do with that piece by Beethoven?"

CHAPTER FOUR

"IT IS A GOOD THING, my dear, that I have brought some of that Constantia wine with me that so used to help Mr. Jennings' colicky gout, as you look sadly pale. I'm sure a glass of that must put you to rights as soon as may be. Lord, but I declare you are wasting away and it will not do."

Mrs. Jennings could not be accused of doing the same thing herself. In seven years, she had increased in girth. Now she had to pause for breath, but her twinkling eyes, as she held Marianne at arm's length, showed how busy her mind was.

"Yes, Ma'am," was all that Marianne said, but her smile reached her eyes. Once, it had taken all Elinor's persuasion to make the seventeen-year-old Marianne civil to Mrs. Jennings.

Since then, she had come to value the widow's good heart, and to gloss over her vulgarities with far more affection than her elder daughter.

"Though you may not be willing to go in society as yet, I am sure there can be no objection to your taking part in family amusements. Ain't that so, Sir John?"

"Aye, certainly, Ma'am. Mrs. Brandon must not become a recluse," replied her son-in-law, who had learned the meaning of the word from his wife, and had taken to it. "Would not do at all. Brandon wouldn't have said it was right, neither."

He broke off here, his youngest son having run in and claimed his attention by kicking him as hard as he could on the shin. Sir John let out a delighted shout of laughter, and Lady Middleton observed, "Little Henry is so bold."

Little Henry furthered the impression by wandering about the room roaring unrestrainedly. To be fair to the infant, he may have been trying to sing, for the younger Middletons seemed to have less of a musical ear than Sir John himself, while their mother had given up practicing music from the day of her marriage.

The door burst open and the older sons came shouting into the room, creating such uproar that even Sir John noticed it. "Quiet or I'll thrash the lot of you!" he cried.

This promise, though often made, was never kept: it had ceased to be anything but a mild deterrent to any but the youngest. He, however, rushed to his mother's skirts, bursting into howls that surpassed the noise before.

Marianne thought it did her good to visit the Middleton family. She never left without feeling that her own regrets over the childlessness of her union with Colonel Brandon were exaggerated. Whereas, when she visited Elinor and Edward, she felt it keenly.

Here Lady Middleton exerted herself. Though still an indulgent mother, she had become a valetudinarian since the birth of her last child. She now objected to shouting from the children – enjoyable as it must be for their guests – as bad for her own health.

She rose from her *chaise longue* to ring for the nurse. The children were taken away for treats. Their distant yells sounded down the corridor, and as Mrs. Jennings accompanied them, the room settled into quiet.

Lady Middleton here honoured her visitor with some conversation. "Dear me, Mrs Brandon, you have no notion of how difficult matters have become for me since my maid Hogg became rheumatic. It is really too bad of her, when I suffer so much from my own afflictions. I am sure I don't know who else to have visit in the village. I used to send her when Sir John wished to have some misfortune of the villagers looked into, and now she insists it is beyond her."

Here Sir John made some bluff remark about how getting out into the fresh air more would soon set to rights both Mrs. Hogg's rheumatics and Lady Middleton's own nervous palpitations and the aching in her ankles.

Lady Middleton frowned. She was happy to suggest that remedy to Hogg, but she felt it insensitive with regard to herself. Besides, it was improper for Sir John to refer to her ankles in company.

Marianne said, "Indeed, Ma'am, if you would not consider it an impertinence, I would be happy to assist you in this matter. I used to help the Colonel and my sister at Delaford with the visiting in the villages. Now I have so much time on my hands that I would be happy to do what I could to fill

Mrs. Hogg's place as your emissary."

Sir John clapped his hands and promised to introduce Marianne to his steward to take her on a round of the village soon as was convenient to Marianne. Hogg was a capital fellow, and had all the rights of the matter.

Lady Middleton was pleased enough to smile. Her languid thanks were cut off by Mrs. Jennings' coming back with the Constantia wine, insisting that both Marianne and her daughter take a glass.

Marianne's meeting with Sir John's steward Mr. Hogg– who showed a sympathy with his name in his avoirdupois and his little, shrewd, deeply buried eyes – took place a couple of days later. He was to show her over the villages. Sir John had great faith in him, and Marianne found herself distrusting him at once. He had a sly, conniving look, and a habit of flattery.

Sir John was good humoured and generous by nature. To stint his tenants and labourers, had he known that they were in any want, would be totally alien to him. Likewise, his wife, if not motivated by generous feeling, had no wish to appear mean, and therefore, vulgar. There were enough funds provided for the tenants to have no fear of want. Yet, something was amiss.

Sir John, of course, never visited in the villages. He was too occupied with sport and in entertaining for his acquaintance. Yet, on riding past various cottages he could not fail to notice now and then, that this wall was in urgent need of repair, or that child was noticeably ragged.

He reported these matters for his steward to investigate, or Mrs. Hogg, Lady Middleton's now ailing lady's maid. Still, somehow, nothing seemed to come of it all. The wall stayed at a crazy angle, and the child remained in rags. Mr. Hogg, if questioned, assured Sir John that offers had been made or funds provided, but that the family were a poor lot and more or less beyond help.

Marianne sensed that Mr. Hogg resented any interference in the running of the funds set aside for such matters, though he hid this from his undiscerning master. Marianne feared that Sir John's steward hoodwinked him often. Still, in accordance with the fair mindedness which Elinor, Edward and Colonel Bandon had urged on her these last few years, she resolved to give the man the benefit of the doubt.

Accordingly, she accepted as graciously as she could Mr. Hogg's proposal that he drive her to the village and introduce her to the tenants the next day.

Mr. Hogg called the next morning in his dog cart to drive Marianne to the village. She was deliberately wearing an old gown, and so had no concerns – save for the extra work for the woman who came in to do the laundry –if it was splashed by the wheel, for it had rained in the night, and the ruts in the lane were full of puddles as they bowled along to the village.

The fresh morning warmed in the sunshine; the birds sang loud, and she felt her spirits rising. This

came as a pleasant surprise. Since the Colonel's
death, fair and foul weather had been alike to her.

This lightening of her mood was despite her
company. She found Mr. Hogg by no means a pleasant companion. Almost every word that he said
showed his ignorance. His education was largely
not his fault, but his shiftiness was. This repelled
her, and she wondered all over again, as she had so
often in the past, at Sir John's undiscerning nature.

When they arrived in the village, Mr. Hogg
handed her down with ceremony, and Marianne
glanced about. She had rarely walked into the village on her visits here.

Barton was in most ways a stereotypical village.
There was green with a pond; there was an inn, a
farrier's, a couple of small shops and other varied
amenities. The church stood some way outside the
village, and among its outbuildings one was allo-
cated to a dame school. The houses varied from
respectable cottages to ramshackle hovels not
much larger than shacks.

Even with the tenants on the land of her enlight-
ened Colonel, Marianne had always been shocked
by the cramped conditions in which the labour-
ing classes lived, their daily fight against want, the
draughts and damp that the most careful landlord
could not eradicate from their poorly made dwellings, the smokiness of their chimneys, and the
unrelenting monotony of their diet.

She expected to find much the same here, and
to do what she could to relieve the lot of any who
were suffering from the added misfortune of infir-
mity or bereavement, and if she saw the need for
some essential repair, to send word for it to be done.

Some ragged children played together over by the village green. Seeing her glance at them, her escort hurried her away from them and into one of the more spacious, well- maintained cottages, where they were greeted by a servile woman in a mob cap.

This woman, whose husband worked as carpenter, had a kitchen newly swept, and a notably fine dresser with pots and pans hanging shining from hooks. Her very children, in their docility, seemed designed as an ideal example – and as unlike the Middletons' own as can be imagined.

She assured Marianne that she had everything that she could require and that Sir John and his steward were all that was generous. She finished every sentence with a curtsey and, 'An' it please you, Ma'am – Sir.' Marianne supposed her family to be the model tenants of which each village has an example.

They passed on to another house, Mr. Hogg hurrying Marianne past a toothless old woman at the door of one of the less picturesque dwellings in the road, past a shop where the proprietor touched his forelock and on to another cottage on the road out of the village.

Here the housewife had much the same story to tell as the first. This was interrupted now and then by her old father, who sat by the fireplace, Bible in hand, airing judgements on his neighbours, whom he dismissed as shiftless and worldly.

"A poor lot they be, a poor lot. Too much liking for cider and not enough thought for their final destination."

Coming out, they saw lounging up across the

street a shiftless looking man, whose own destination seemed to be the village tavern. Mr. Hogg
clicked his tongue and put his bulk between Marianne and this sight.

The man went into the taproom of the inn and
Mr. Hogg stopped to exchange a few words with
the landlord outside, who bowed to Marianne.

After this, Mr. Hogg seemed to regard Marianne's
visit to be completed. "So you see, people here do
well enough. Hard work brings its own rewards. At
least, that's what I learned when I was a lad, and so
it is here. There is another of His Honour's tenants
I'd like you for to meet, as he lives on the way out
of the village. Then we can make for Barton Cottage via the top lane."

He drew back when she said, "Thank you, Mr.
Hogg; you have been all kindness in showing me
about. Now I will take up no more of your time,
as I am sure you have much to do. Barton Cottage
is within easy walking distance, and I will have no
trouble in making my own way back. I would like
to meet more of the villagers."

Mr. Hogg drew back, protesting: 'Indeed, Ma'am,
I would scarce recommend it. Some of them villagers be a rough lot. You've seen Tom Harvey, and
he's not the worst. Their places are not fit to be
seen, and through their own shiftless natures live
little better than animals; happen you'd have a nasty
shock, Ma'am, and that's a fact."

Marianne was inclined to laugh. "I can endure a
little squalor without any danger to my nerves, and
I am sure that Sir John's tenants will be civil to his
emissary."

Mr. Hogg frowned at that word. Though unsure

of its meaning, he was certain its use boded ill for him. "I should hope not indeed, Ma'am. But you will exhaust yourself. If you were to name another day, I should be happy to introduce you to a couple of the other cots out of the way."

Marianne laughed at the idea of being exhausted. She had so often visited in the village at Delaford. Mr. Hogg continued to protest, even invoking the threat of rain later in the day, although there were few clouds in the sky. But Marianne was obdurate, and he had to take his leave.

Marianne now visited a couple of the dwellings which Mr. Hogg had not shown her. She did not visit the most ramshackle, as, through a sense of the dramatic, she would have done as a young girl. Instead, she aimed for ones neither superior nor amongst the most miserable. She called in at a cottage, which, though minute and comfortless enough by her own standards, looked well maintained, while behind she could see a recently turned over vegetable patch.

Marianne went up to the door, where the goodwife was standing in talk with her neighbour. As they made their curtseys, she introduced herself.

The woman seemed unnerved to speak to a member of the gentry. However, her neighbour said at once how surprised she was that anyone but 'Them Planks and them others' should receive a visit, as 'They be in with the steward, and gets the best of everything, whiles other folk must get on as best they can.'

"I am sorry to hear that has been your experience, and am here to see if anyone is in distress," said Marianne, going on to explain how she came to replace Mrs. Hogg.

The women exchanged a look far from compli-
mentary to Mrs. Hogg, and the first woman said,
"Of course, you be very welcome to enter, Mum,
though it's not at all what you are used to. Perhaps
you would be good enough to tell me what you
make of my Tommy's chest."

Marianne was happy to step in. The inside of the
cottage showed that the woman laboured to try
and keep it clean and neat, while a large pan of
potatoes bubbling over the fire would be the main
part of the family's dinner. The fire itself smoked
dismally into the room, as with so many of the
cottages. Marianne, struggling against a coughing
fit, could not wonder that infant crawling on the
floor had a bad chest.

Following the ideas which she had from the local
apothecary and which had benefited the villagers
at Delaford, Marianne advised the woman to keep
him out in the fresh air as much as possible in dry
weather. She left the woman some of her tincture
and the soup from her basket.

She asked her to let her know of other cases
where help was needed, and the woman became
almost loquacious. Though Marianne doubted the
powers of either herself and Sir John, let alone Mr.
Hogg, to mend the heart of young Harvey's wife
– broken since he had turned to idle ways – or
that of his aged mother, who could no longer hold
up her head in the village – she thought that she
could at least do something to help his family stave
off want.

Marianne knew it was the practice of many of
her fellows to provide only for the deserving poor.

However, the truly charitable Edward and Elinor Ferrars had always held that the family of an undeserving man suffered no less from hunger and cold than that of a diligent though unlucky citizen. Perhaps they suffered more, for they had the scorn of their neighbours to contend with besides.

Accordingly, they always held that it was doubly a Christian duty to help in such cases, while trying to ensure that they did nothing to encourage the erring man's shiftless ways, and tried by exhortation to discourage them.

Marianne was relieved that young Harvey was still away from his comfortless dwelling, though his wife and mother were home. She doubted her ability to make him see the error of his ways through words, if only because he had looked well in his cups. She left soup with these women, too, and even some of her tincture, for the old mother seemed to covet this as a cure all in the same light as Mrs. Jennings' Constantia wine (and no doubt young Harvey would have greatly preferred some of that).

The inside of the cottage was bare, stuffy and dismal, and Marianne was glad to escape from it to the fresh air outside.

She needed only a short talk with these women to add more to her suspicions that Mr. Hogg unfairly used funds Sir John set aside for charity, with the bulk of it going to a favoured few and the rest into his own pockets. This was an old story, after all. Marianne had heard tales of such mean corruption since her childhood, but somehow had never thought to come across evidence of it on the estates of her friends.

As she began on the walk home from the village, she puzzled over what best to do. To confront Mr. Hogg or his patron was unwise until she learned more of what was happening.

Now, she felt the extent of her loss in Colonel Brandon all over again. She had been in the habit of taking moral quandaries to him. He always seemed to know how best to act in such cases. After all, he was a military man and had the air of authority and the habit of command she lacked.

Thinking over these matters as she walked up the lane, Marianne was only dimly aware of her surroundings. She had just resolved to write, asking Elinor and Edward for their advice, when she heard the approach of a rider. Looking up, saw Willoughby coming her way.

CHAPTER FIVE

HER FIRST THOUGHT, ABSURDLY, WAS of flight or concealment; but this was impossible. He had seen her, and she could hardly pretend she had missed seeing him. She stayed where she was while he rode up, showing all the dash in his style, the easy mastery of his mount that had once sent shivers of admiration up her spine.

He made her his bow with the same easy grace as ever.

"Mr. Willoughby." She greeted him coldly enough.

He was smiling at her, eyes sparkling with the same admiration. "I have been longing to see you again."

She had to admit he looked very well; how he managed to do so, leading the life style he did, was a mystery.

"If, Sir, that was because you wished to apologise for your freedoms when last we met −" she began.

"I can't apologise for them; I don't regret them. Mrs. Brandon − Good God, how I hate calling you that! Please don't flounce off in anger. I have admitted Colonel Brandon to be a far better man than I am, and thoroughly deserving of your regard, after all. Still I cannot help envying him your good opinion, and I want to call you my love, as you are."

"Sir, I must bid you good day." She turned to leave.

He put a hand on her arm to detain her. She paused under his touch and his old, beguiling look and the engaging air that urged her to forgive the improprieties of his conduct.

No doubt it had worked so on Eliza, to her downfall.

He laughed then. "This is again like to that terrible day when I thought you dying, and rode like the devil to burst in on your sister, who thought me drunk. No, Ma'am – is that formal enough? – I am as miserably sober now as I was then. I only take too much in Town, so as to keep up the appearance of the high spirits that once I had. If only you will stay, I will try to be reasonable."

"I suppose I have no choice, Sir." Marianne surrendered her basket to him. They walked on together, with him leading his horse.

"Is Mrs. Willoughby with you?" she asked coolly.

"No," he looked not in the least abashed, "She and Mrs. Smith don't agree; they found that out soon enough. The old lady is feeble now, and scarce leaves her room. The doctor forever prescribes this or that draught, and it has come to her refusing to take any of them, save if I cajole her, and I came up in part for that purpose. I won't deny the other part had something to do with hearing you were in the area."

He looked at her meaningfully. She ignored his

glance, and he went on, "I know I owe her every attention, as she has made me her heir, and been good to me in her own, narrow way. Now I find that when I come to inherit –which in the nature of things cannot be many years –I must regret her loss. You may be dismayed to hear that for long, I blamed her for my unlucky marriage, and that did away with any affection I had previously had for her." This was said with all the appearance of reckless honesty he had of old.

Marianne said in measured tones, "Mr. Willoughby, on our last meeting, you mentioned the advice my sister gave to you, and wise advice it was, particularly from a nineteen-year-old."

He smiled, and against her will, the corners of her lips turned slightly upwards in response. "Elinor was always correct in every sense. I know I should have done as she urged then, but it is too difficult. Through my own folly I have harnessed myself with a woman with the temper of a vixen, but it is too damned much to hear you – of all people – urging my duty on me. Well, I suppose you've heard some fine stories of me, both old and new."

Looking at her still, he sighed, and then reddened. "Ah, yes, I have been bad enough, and worst of all was my treatment of poor Eliza. You are hardly likely to overlook that, when you must often have met, and she will have told you her version of the story, with me as the heartless libertine, and she as injured innocence."

Marianne said coldly, "I did meet her. I am sure you will have heard that a respectable man had formed an attachment to her, which she returned.

They are now married, and he has been unusual in wishing to raise the child as his own."

Willoughby scowled. "I do not know if you heard I offered her assistance when finally I heard of the child. I was cursed out of pocket, but I would have raised the money – but the Colonel would never allow me to do anything for them, even after our duel. I am sure you know that I am not permitted to see the child, who may well be my only one."

Marianne did not say, 'So it is to be hoped' or 'To your knowledge'. She did say, "I believe that the girl was only fifteen when you seduced her."

"No, Marianne – I mean Mrs. Brandon – she was the grand old age of sixteen. But I make no excuse for myself, for none can be made, save to say that I forgot to give the girl my direction when I left, though, as I told your sister, through using some common sense she could easily have found out my whereabouts when she learned of her condition."

Marianne remained silent. She had sometimes wondered if the Colonel was unjust in refusing Willoughby any chance of making such reparation to Eliza and her child as was in his power.

Previously, she had tended to take on trust his own view of the matter, that little Betty should not be in contact with her natural father, unprincipled libertine as he had proved himself to be. Marianne had seen the wisdom of this. Seeing that the child had a step-father who was fond of her, any inter-vention from Eliza's old seducer seemed intrusive and unfortunate.

Now, she frowned, puzzling over it all. She had an uneasy sense that while the Colonel had acted correctly according to his code of honour and decorum, in some ways these were too strictly conventional, and accordingly lacking in a flexible acceptance of human frailty. Eliza was forgiven by her guardian, but never again had been permitted to appear in polite society.

Colonel Brandon would have argued that, as society would not accept her, this was the best course to take. But Marianne couldn't help thinking that he saw Eliza, through her fall from virtue at Willoughby's hands, as being a possible bad influence on other young girls. The man who had married her, however much her superior in understanding, was her social inferior, though he had used his army connections as a means to improve himself.

As all this passed through Marianne's mind, Willoughby was still looking at her with such a look of yearning as to make her bite her lip and say briskly, "It is all very sad. Still, we cannot undo the past, Mr. Willoughby. We can only make resolutions with regard to the future."

"Mine will be bleak enough, if you form no part of it," he returned.

She reached to take the basket from him, saying almost wearily, "Sir, you know how insulting such a line of talk is, to me, to the memory of Colonel Brandon, and to your wife, and yet you persist in it. Once again, I must bid you goodbye."

"Wait! If you leave now, you leave taking me to task only half done." He smiled, and absurdly she found her indignation melting.

She said, "There isn't much more that I can say to you, Sir. You cultivate, and express feelings for me that you cannot fail to know you should not. As a married man, your intentions towards me can never be honourable."

"If I were ever free —" he began.

"It is very wrong to speak so."

"It may be wrong, but it is only damned natural. If I were free, and approached you at a later date, when you had mourned Brandon long enough to satisfy you, would you dismiss me? I know I am unworthy of you; I have been bad enough; I betrayed you for material gain, and you know the worst I have done in ruining poor Eliza. Well, I am justly punished; all my present misfortunes stem from that. But had I acted other than as a fool back in those days, and married you as I always at heart wanted, then I would never have fallen so low."

His eyes caught hers, and hers must have revealed far more than she imagined was there, for he sighed even as she returned, "Mr. Willoughby, it outrages every proper notion to talk on these lines. But I will answer you, despite that. Even if we were both free, I could not consider a man of libertine practices. I am sorry to speak so indelicately and so ungraciously, though you force me to it."

At her words, he drew back, wincing, and came to a stop. "There was a time when you might have considered it romantic to hazard your happiness with such a one."

She felt the colour flame to her cheeks still more. "No, Sir; as a young girl my ideas were far too idealistic for that."

He sighed, shaking his head. "I have not forgotten your ideals. I recall all your ideas more vividly than you can imagine. I remember, too, how you denied the possibility of second attachments. In that, the libertine proved himself a greater romantic than the innocent. You lived to disprove your own dictates, and find marital happiness with the Colonel, whereas I have not had any other love but the one I had for you. You draw back. But it is so."

She had to concede this. Ironically, he, with his outrageous reputation, had been the one whose feelings for his first genuine attachment – herself – had never altered. Apart from the short weeks of assumed indifference after he had publicly jilted her and was courting Miss Grey, he had been constant in his regret at losing Marianne. He had never made more than the feeblest attempt to hide his continuing passion for her. She, by contrast, had found comfort with Colonel Brandon and four years of marital happiness.

She brooded over what best to urge on Willoughby, until seeing his look of unrestrained longing, and realising that they should not be standing here together alone, she began to walk on, with him walking on besides her.

Their being together felt entirely natural. Worse, this wholly improper talk between them was coming to feel so too. In the days when he had been courting her, they had always been straightforward with each other, and as their views generally coincided, this had never led to disputes.

She turned over in her mind how best to try and bring home to him the wrong he was doing them all. She was deterred by having no wish to speak of her own recent loss to one who had never valued the Colonel as he deserved, and who even now resented what he saw as an injustice at his hands, when truly the worst injustice had been that done by himself to Brandon's ward.

Finally, she said, "When I urge your duty on you, I am not taking an uncritical view of my own conduct under my recent misfortune, which has been far from exemplary. I hope I do not sound sententious; but I must speak as candidly as you seem to demand."

She bit her lip. "Forgive me; – but you squander your talents, and live in discord with your wife. Yet surely, it would be more comfortable for you –leaving aside the ethics of the matter – at least to be on more amiable terms with her? I cannot believe that to be impossible, when once she was sufficiently attached to you to have her friends promote the match, and after all, you were able to regard your future with her with some complacency."

He came to an abrupt halt, eyes sparking, though whether through resentment, passion or amusement, or some mixture of all three, she could not tell. "I am deservedly rebuked. It would be ridiculous to deny that I lead a sorry life. But I must see the influence of your excellent sister and Mr. Ferrars in this piece of high falutin' advice. The Marianne Dashwood of old could never have made that speech."

Marianne wondered about this herself. It was bad enough having not only to guard against giving in to a resurgence of her old feelings for him; but to struggle against these, and to keep him at a respectable distance, too, was exhausting.

She felt in danger of being overwhelmed by the flood of emotions that his closeness and passionate words roused in her. His tone, his glance, his words, aroused old associations and an old sorrow that she had thought long forgotten.

She had again to bite her trembling lip before replying. "If I could not, then so much the worse for me, though I hope that is not true. But do you know that I quite envy you, Sir? You are in the position to accomplish so much. When I was mistress at Delaford, I could visit the villagers, and so make some improvement in their lives. You are heir to Mrs. Smith's estate, and as she is now so much retired, I am sure she would appreciate your help in the running of it, and bettering the lot of the tenants. If you cannot think of improving matters with your wife, then at least, when it comes to these other responsibilities —"

"Not another word, damn it!" he exclaimed, coming again to a stop and turning on her in a fury she had never seen in him before. "I cannot endure to hear this from you, of all people. As to my wife, it must come to a separation; we are so at each other's throats. Then, Mrs. Brandon, you recommend to me a life devoted to duty?"

He stood breathing quickly, while unseen by either of them, a hare bolted across their path. Willoughby's normally fractious mount did not even notice. Throughout their talk, it had showed remarkable patience at being stopped and started at every other minute, and now stood gently waving its ears, almost as if it felt for its master's desperation.

He rushed on, "No doubt that is how you plan to waste your youth and beauty. No, I cannot find comfort in a life devoted to good works. Mrs. Smith's tenants must go to hell in a handcart along with their master, when he comes to inherit. Lord, but I am well served for my former misdeeds and treachery."

He gazed at her wildly, and she stood, wondering if she looked like a transfixed rabbit, as he went on, "Hear me, Marianne: I *will* call you that: you were devoted to the excellent Colonel –Ah, what a lucky man he was. – I would willingly swap places with him, and be underground now, for having had the bliss of four years with you. *He* only suffered from the misery of seeing you with another for a few short weeks.

'You look your rebuke, and not only for my poor taste in speaking to you so when you have been under a year a widow, but for my histrionic words. Soon I will be ranting of thunderbolts and daggers and a life of living hell…Your heightened colour recalls to me the former Marianne Dashwood. Well, I'm to Town tomorrow. Perhaps you will rejoice that I go? A word of regret from you will detain me."

Dismayed at how breathless her voice was, she retorted, "For which reason, Mr. Willoughby, I must say none. But please believe me, I wish you happier, and Mrs. Willoughby, too. I am heartily sorry that you see my words as so much empty sententiousness."

He sighed again. "I will leave you now, for we approach Barton Cottage. I shall not ask you to give my compliments to Mrs. Dashwood, as she has had the excellent taste to abhor me every since I betrayed you. Goodbye."

He handed over her basket, kissed her hand with lips that burnt fully as much as any of those of the heroes in the novels he so despised, and jumped on his horse, which, restored to normal behaviour, flung its head and snorted. Wheeling it about, he urged it into a gallop and was gone.

Left by herself, Marianne went to sit on a stile nearby as she regained enough equanimity to appear calm when she met her family. This took some while, as her heart was both full of indignation at Willoughby's words and sympathy for him, and her colour came and went as she thought over their exchanges.

She had no doubt at all, that had she given him the slightest encouragement, he would have come back to her in due course, to urge her to go away with him, and to live with him outside marriage.

Her family and friends would be speechless with indignation if they knew; her late beloved Colonel would –could he possibly have known – been roused to fury. Alive, he would as a matter of course have proposed another duel with Willoughby.

Yet, Marianne herself could not be as indignant with him as she should. Her views had changed since she was an idealistic girl. She was even unorthodox in her views on marriage in a way that would have shocked the Colonel more than Willoughby's intentions. Now she felt that those who insisted on the indissolubility of marriage were wrong, and that where the partners were truly incompatible, there should be more provision for divorce.

Had it been possible for Willoughby to have divorced his wife and to offer to marry her, would she have agreed to it? She had told him that was out of the question, due to his libertine propensities; that was the truth in so far as she knew it herself. Still, she had reason to doubt her resolution in the weak feelings with which he had let her. She

suspected that he would, with time and persistence
–accompanied, of course, with specious offers of
reformation – have worn down her resistance. It
was, probably lucky that divorce was almost a prac-
tical impossibility, so that she would never be tried.

She sighed when she thought of poor Mrs. Willoughby, who had once been so jealous that she
had dictated that callous letter to Marianne with
which he had rejected her. But Willoughby would
not hear Marianne's counsel on his treatment of his
wife any more than he had once heeded Elinor's.

Then Marianne smiled, remembering herself as
a young girl, refusing to believe in second attachments. Willoughby had anyway been in the right
about that; she had lived to prove herself wrong
and be happy with the Colonel. Ironically, the libertine had lived up to her dictates, never making
any secret of the fact that Marianne was the only
woman he had loved, even devoting more energy
than tact in convincing his wife of that.

CHAPTER SIX

WILLOUGHBY ARRIVED BACK IN LON-
DON with all his usual vigour, yelling to
the grooms and striding into the house. He only
paused to pass an amiable comment to the footmen before charging up the stairs, shouting for his
valet.

His wife heard his arrival from her dressing
room, where she was putting on her new dam-
ask silk gown, which she thought became her. She
trembled and blushed like a bride. Still, she pulled a
sour face to try and disguise it from her maid.

The valet, though he talked more about his
errant master than he should, worshipped him, and
responded to his summons with a grin.

Spencer had been obliged to stay at home
through slipping on the front stairs and spraining
his ankle. This accident inspired some bitter wit
from Willoughby. "For the future, stick to the back
stairs, if these front ones are so slippery. I mind me,
someone else once fell and twisted her ankle, but
it was a sight prettier than yours, so you don't need
to think I'll carry you," he advised his man, as he

hobbled into the room, complaining of the treach-
erous stairs.

"It's a fine thing to see you back, Sir," Spencer
said more than once, as he helped Willoughby
ready himself for dinner at top speed.

"Given how things have been between my nem-
esis and me of late, it's no fine damned thing to
be back," muttered Willoughby. He strode down to
dinner only a few minutes late.

His wife was already in her place, and she flushed
again and her hands clenched at her napkin as Willoughby made his bow and seated himself.

"How does poor Mrs. Smith?" She tried to inject
a note of concern into her voice, while the man
trod about with the soup.

"She's rallying; she'll do well enough," Willoughby replied promptly. This was not true; he
knew Mrs. Smith to be still ailing. Still, as his wife,
who longed to take over as mistress of Allenham,
wanted confirmation of this, he treated it almost as
his duty to disappoint her. "Thank you," he turned
a warm smile on the footman.

Mrs. Willoughby tried not to frown. In this
household, the wife often had fewer smiles than
the servants, so she could hardly be surprised by
it. Nevertheless, it still had power to make her
wretched.

She retreated into quietness, for she was still
determined to keep to her resolve not to quarrel
with him. For his part, Willoughby was not a man
to whom it was natural to be taciturn. He talked of
Sir John's new hunter and his game birds. He failed
to notice her new gown; that was typical of a man,
but she was disappointed still.

She had, as ever, missed him in his absence. Then, as so often before, she had made a resolution to try and improve relations with him by checking her own hasty temper and meeting his misconduct with restraint.

It would be untrue to say that they had never lived in harmony. The pattern of their married life was one where periods of relative quiet and mutual tolerance —while she allowed him to go his own way, and he kept her content enough for them to live in relative calm —alternated with ones of marital strife, open dispute, and undignified scenes.

Willoughby was carelessly good natured by disposition; he was not often actively unkind to his wife. She remained as hopelessly in love with him as she had always been since first they met, but hers was a grudge bearing disposition; she remembered insulting comments he had made – and particularly invidious comparisons he had made between herself and the now Mrs. Brandon – with the bitterest clarity.

Since their marriage, he had made little effort to conceal from her that he had married her for her money, and for some reason this candour did not have the effect of endearing him to her.

At least, Willoughby had not been altogether hypocritical about this before their wedding. One night shortly before their union, when he had taken too much wine, he had told her with more enthusiasm than tact that: "He needed her fortune like the devil but could never give his heart to anyone but Marianne Dashwood, and that as he could not abandon his dissolute way of life, she must come to hate him."

The then Sophia Grey had laughed at this. "She would tame him, and make domestic life so appealing that he would have no wish to go upon the Town."

She had also believed that he must in time come to love her, though she hadn't confided this fancy to him or to anyone else. Though she had long since lost her illusions regarding this, she was unable to stop being in love with him. She was, however, aware, when not actively angry with him, that he had become accustomed to her, and in the course of time, even carelessly fond of her, at least during their periods of reasonable contentment.

Over the last year, however, the death of Colonel Brandon had increased Willoughby's latent dissatisfaction with his wife to fever pitch. It spurred him to provoking behaviour that would have tried the patience of a nature far sweeter than hers. This had led at last to the degrading quarrel in their curricle so faithfully reported by Miss Steele.

This evening, for once, they had no guests to dinner. One or more of Willoughby's ubiquitous group of friends habitually came to dine, for they considered themselves to have standing invitations. Sometimes their wives came as well. 'Company for you, my dear,' said Willoughby. Sophia Willoughby often invited her own guests, and friends they had in common came regularly, too – but tonight, she had made no arrangements herself, and Willoughby, having arrived back in Town just before the meal, had no time to make any of his own to dilute her company.

His handsome looks and that indefinable charm of glance and manner as he sat across the table from her, talking idly of this or that – this man who was hers, but never hers – provoked her to silent resentment. What did he mean by looking so bright eyed, glowing, healthy and athletic after so many years of leading such a life?

However, she tried for an amiable tone. "And how do the Middletons, besides Sir John's new horse?"

"As stupid as ever. Lord knows how Mrs. Jennings' tongue hasn't worn out by this." Willoughby had never cared about discretion before the servants.

It had come to Mrs. Willoughby's hearing that Colonel Brandon's widow was back at Barton, and this had added to her anxiety for his return. Marianne's presence haunted the meal, though her name remained unspoken.

Just as Marianne herself regarded mention of the Colonel's name before his old opponent Willoughby as somehow cheapening the regard that she had for him, so Willoughby saw speaking of the former Marianne Dashwood to his wife in the same light.

Accordingly, her name was only raised during quarrels. Then Willoughby was eager to restore marital harmony by making those invidious comparisons regarding the temper, understanding and beauty of the two, while his final attempt at conciliation was to enlighten his wife about the amount of love he had ever felt for each or could ever feel in the future.

During heated disputes in the past, Willoughby had pointed out the deficiencies of his wife's complexion as lacking in natural bloom. Since this ungallant criticism, she had used a good deal of tincture of Benjoin, Gowland's Lotion and Pimpernel Water, with little effect. She also applied rouge discreetly, which had more. This was especially necessary to her on the days when she had taken too much wine the night before. Those days, sadly, were becoming more frequent.

On the few occasions when Mrs. Willoughby had seen the former Marianne Dashwood in town, she had gazed on her so as to take in the minutest details of her face, dress and figure. Had she possessed the artistic flair of the now Elinor Ferrars, she could have drawn her from memory. Naturally, she had paid keen attention to any faults. She had regarded it as her duty to correct Willoughby's mistaken belief that the now Mrs. Brandon was as beautiful as any angel.

He, far from being grateful, had been inclined to slam out of the room with a muttered insult about 'jealous females'.

Now, Sophie Willoughby thrust back thoughts of the widowed Mrs. Brandon and did her best to smile on her errant spouse. Sometimes, when in high good humour with her, when the footmen's backs were turned, he quickly –and with shocking impropriety – saluted her lips when she left him to his port, and she hoped he would do so this evening. She thought of his strong arm drawing her to his athletic form, and looked forward to his coming to her bed tonight. She would leave her doors temptingly ajar, for he had at least kept to his side of their bargain in that.

Sophia Willoughby's resolution to promote marital harmony proved as short lived as her previous ones, particularly as Willoughby himself did little to encourage it. He was in a mood both wild and reckless. He went back to his dissolute ways with the vigour he brought to everything.

As always, her friends during her hours at home once again cast her looks of pity. Everyone had heard of how he had been seen handing down *Signora* Lucasta from her carriage, and how he had quarrelled violently over cards at the *Star and Garter*. She herself tried to ignore it, though she heard enough to make her red with mortification. She wondered at the rogue's energy —he was after all, thirty – and she wondered the more, as in recent weeks her own had been so depleted.

This had at least one good effect; constant quarrelling with Willoughby over his outrages seemed after all to require too much effort. Now, she told him that he was, "A wretch, but after all, what could she expect, when she had shown so little sense as to marry a self-confessed fortune hunter" only once a week.

She had seen her physicians about this increasing malaise, her breathlessness and dizzy spells, and been prescribed draughts that were of no use. She was out of patience with them all; she consulted another, who was no more helpful. She caught him, as she thought, looking at her oddly – it seemed to her, almost with compassion – and such a look was not common among fashionable doctors, whose chief concern was for their fee.

She caught a glimpse of her face in the looking glass in which she had seen him admiring himself as she came in for her consultation. Her complexion looked more sallow than ever, she thought, and she left in high ill humour.

That night, her maid had to apply a good deal of rogue to pass her off as looking even tolerably healthy. She and Willoughby went to an assembly. Here he seemed to make a point of being provoking. He was animated with every dance partner save herself, and he flirted openly with their hostess, who tittered and tossed her head infuriatingly.

Mrs. Willoughby drank some wine, but it failed to lighten her mood, though it did make her giddy. Having no wish to be thought in her cups when she was sober, she left early in their carriage, while Willoughby went with a couple of friends to see if he could further blacken his reputation.

Arriving home, she lost a shoe getting out of the carriage. The bitter irony of any association with the Cinderella story was not lost on her. She made no attempt to look for it, leaving that to the coachman, and stumbled into her hallway, where she cast the other in a corner, and stormed up the stairs.

Halfway up, she was overcome by a fit of her recurrent breathlessness, which brought on a wave of dizziness. Clutching at the banister, her fingers slid along its polished length, even as her stockimged feet slipped on the stairs, and with a muffled cry, she plunged into blackness.

CHAPTER SEVEN

M RS. WILLOUGHBY'S FAVOURITE DOC-
TOR LIVED in the same street; he came
speedily, happening to be at home. He diagnosed
a fracture to the limb. Despite his habitual air of
serene optimism, secretly he took a dim view of
the case.

Willoughby's valet Spencer saw this from the
very tilt of the physician's head as he came out
onto the landing, with orders for one of the men
to run for a colleague. Knowing his master's temperament better than Willoughby himself, Spencer
went out in search of him.

If a certain interest in the gentry's exclusive and
dissolute haunts of pleasure played a part in Spencer's anxiety to trace his master, it was only a part.
He knew Willoughby would be concerned at the
danger to his termagant of a wife. He had seen
them fond enough at times, when they were not
quarrelling about what seemed to him to be nothing of much import, what with there being more
than enough money to keep them both happy,
though to be sure there were no young 'uns, and

the years hadn't lessened Willoughby's urge to go on the town.

Had the stakes not been so high in the Cocoa Tree, Spencer might have lingered there, in the hope that they might take money from a menial; but recalled from gazing longingly at the tables, he went on to the next of Willoughby's favourite haunts, to which he had been overheard directing the coachman. He only missed him by some minutes, and so went on to the next, which Willoughby had just left in turn.

As the night wore on, Spencer at last concluded that Willoughby had gone to end his revels in the company of a woman of questionable character. At last, he abandoned the chase, having left messages that Mrs. Willoughby had suffered an accident and was in danger of her life.

He arrived back home not long before dawn. He paused in the hallway at the sound of carriage wheels and a familiar voice outside, and someone springing up the front steps.

Willoughby bounced in, looking as fresh, youthful and untroubled as if he had been for a country walk.

He paused, startled to see Spencer there: "Why the funereal look?"

Spencer was a man with a fine, if uncultivated, feeling for drama. In fact, he had as a boy aspirations to go on the stage. Now, he was able to do full justice to his news. By contorting his face through drawing together his eyebrows, turning down his lips and lengthening his jaw, he contrived to turn his visage into that of a mask of doom.

He intoned on a hollow note, "God be thanked

that you have come, Sir. The mistress has had an accident; and they say that she is in peril of her life."

Willoughby refused to be impressed. He had seen evidence enough, over the years, of his wife's valetudinarianism; she had always been inclined to see herself as mortally afflicted at every slight malaise. But as his man pressed on him the details of Mrs. Willoughby's fall, the fracture, and the physician's sending first for one colleague, and then another, he blanched, beat his forehead with his fist in an manner entirely to his man's satisfaction, finally dashing up the hazardous stairs and cutting off Spencer's words, "We can only pray for her, Sir; she's in God's hands, now."

He paused at the door of his wife's bedchamber, appalled to see her state. Three physicians stood in solemn conference, while she lay back, eyes closed, with the fever already rising to give a sinister flush to her cheeks. This reminded him of former ungallant criticisms he had sometimes made of her sallow complexion, and the first of innumerable shafts of remorse stabbed him so sharply that he drew in his breath through his teeth.

Mrs. Willoughby was still conscious, and in considerable pain. This made her greeting of her errant spouse anything but gracious. "So you're here at last. I won't ask where you've been. It seems you will be rid of me at last; I shan't get the better of this, I can tell."

Willoughby did not at first answer. Instead he put his hands to his face, and groaned aloud. The doctors, who had drawn aside at his entrance, made gestures of warning, which he could not see. They were already agreed between themselves that the patient had an underlying weakness of constitution, which they were willing to ascribe to Willoughby's notorious misconduct. They kept from saying so, however, as his wild look made them fear that he might pitch them down the stairs.

He uncovered his face to wave them away, and they withdrew to the ante room with looks of remonstrance and the two servants.

Willoughby fell on his knees beside his wife's bed in a manner which she would have found delightful, had her own sufferings been little enough for her to appreciate it. She had so long envied Marianne that headlong dash he had made years ago from London to Somersetshire, to what he had thought to be her deathbed.

"Never say so, Sophia," he choked out. "You must live." Taking her too warm hands in his, he gazed on her beseechingly.

"You confuse matters, Sir," even in the physical torment that kept her writhing, Mrs. Willoughby was acid. "I am not the former Marianne Dashwood, but your wife whom you took for her fortune."

"I confuse nothing, you fool, Sophia – we've been together for years, and I must be a monster if I had no warm feelings for you, for all our disputes. I've said so often enough, when we weren't quarrelling."

But even as he spoke, Willoughby realised that he had not said so 'often enough' at all. Instead, he had assumed too readily that she knew that he did not mean what he said in temper, and that he had come to value her. *He* saw their particularly troubled relations in the last few months – in fact, since Mrs. Brandon's widowhood – as being exceptional. *She* might see this conflict as the final result of the uneven feelings between them.

He had an idea that her constant dosing herself with this or that draught might have poisoned her. Still, he could not escape the conviction that his own neglect and indifference – even in their comparatively happy times – hadn't done that more effectively. He could not bear to think of this; it made him feel wild.

As she made no reply, and closed her eyes, he said, "Sophia, is the pain too much? I'll get those cursed useless doctors to give you something further to ease it – but do try and get the better of this."

She still made no reply, and returned to writhing. Willoughby rose unsteadily, and went out to the doctors. They had some medical reasons why they could give Mrs. Willoughby no more draughts to ease her for the moment. He cursed and abused them. They kept their equanimity, perhaps through thinking of their expected fees. They left with dignity, saying that there was nothing more to be done for the present, but promising to return.

An anguished watching followed for Willoughby and his wife. He would not leave her until he saw her sleeping peacefully. This she was unable to do, racked by pain and fever as she was. He was equally racked by guilt and remorse. Both remained sleepless for many hours, while the servants and the doctors came and went.

Willoughby remembered an apothecary of whose draughts Mrs. Willoughby had spoken highly before, and he sent for him, but he was long delayed.

As he sat by her side, Willoughby held himself solely responsible for all their discord, even as prior to her accident, he had been ready to give all the blame to her. His harsh speeches, his habitual indifference, his hateful acts, his life of empty dissipation came back to torment him.

He seemed to himself to be almost a monster, and he writhed in shame. Often, he begged her to forgive him, but she seemed not to hear him. Her words when he had first come in tormented him, and he felt that if she died leaving him like this, he could not face life, weighed down with such a burden of guilt.

Besides, a life without her – which he had sometimes before imagined as a blessing – now seemed unaccountably empty.

He was tormented more than anything by the memory of the abusive things he had said of her to Marianne. He was ashamed besides, because he knew that had Marianne given him the slightest encouragement, he would have done all that he could to persuade her to run away with him. His own reputation was so bad that such an act would do little to make it worse, but the loss of hers would have meant lasting misery for Marianne as well as for Sophia.

His wife had always forgiven him in the past, when contrition on his part had been shallow and ephemeral. Now, she said nothing in reply to his pleas, and he couldn't tell if this was through accident or design.

He took over the role of her nurse, sponging her down with tepid water and coaxing her to drink cordial. His household was amazed; but he had no eyes or ears for them. After some time, he gave up urging her, and tended her in silence.

Finally, she came back to full consciousness and gazed at him some while. "You ask my pardon, as you have so many times before, and thrown it in my face. I have never withheld it yet, and you have it again."

"Thank you, Sophia." He squeezed her hand, sighing in relief. "But if you'll only get the better of this, that will all be in the past. You will see me change. You look disbelieving, my dear, when I've gone back on my word so often. But if only you fight this cursed fracture, you shall see."

"I shall see," was all her response. Still, she added warmth to her words by putting up a hand to caress his face. She had done this often enough in the past, and he had always taken it for granted, but now the tears started to his eyes. Even through the blur in her vision she saw them, and in the middle of her own sufferings, they moved her to magnanimity.

"It was not only you at fault," she said, running her fingers through his hair. "I knew you didn't love me when we married, but I would have you, at any cost. I thought if only you were mine, I'd win your love over time. Well…But in that, I did an injustice to us both."

Her words stopped there, and he broke down entirely; his tears flowed fast. She did not mention the name of Mrs. Brandon *nee* Marianne Dashwood, and neither did he; but now these names were no longer an obstacle between them.

Sophia Willoughby knew that she had at last won

the prize she had so coveted for eight years, ever since she had first met the young Willoughby at an assembly in the company of his bosom companions in Town, Mr. Lequeux and the Honourable William Ashton. Willoughby had made her laugh with a series of witticisms about her former dancing partner's false teeth, periwig and corset.

When he was able to speak, he said, "But I have come to love you, Sophia! I see that clearly, now. Do not let it be too late: it may be a different type of attachment than –than others I have had – but it's no less real. I deserve this hellish guilt. I have been a fool, and I am now well served. I have wasted years, when we could have been happy together."

"You have often been impossible," said Sophia Willoughby, and not without asperity, "Yet, I suppose I did my worst, too." She put up her hand to caress his face again. Then the pain worsened, and she began to writhe.

But now the apothecary arrived, and was able to prescribe a draught that might well sooth the patient and enable her to rest. Shocked at Willoughby's appearance, he went so far as to recommend a draught for him too. He received a reply laced with oaths that only his wife's recovery could do anything for Willoughby himself. This being something about which the apothecary was no more sanguine than the doctors, he left murmuring appropriate phrases, while Mrs. Willoughby at last drifted into sleep.

CHAPTER EIGHT

OVER THE NEXT FEW DAYS, Mrs. Willoughby remained very ill, and usually scarcely conscious. Willoughby spent hours by her bedside, only leaving to snatch a few hours' troubled sleep, or for his joyless solitary mealtimes.

To these, his bosom companions were no longer routine guests. They came now and then, as a sort of duty; still, they found the atmosphere so dismal, and Willoughby so distraught and devoid of his old rattling talk, that they were happy to stay away.

The household was astonished. Willoughby's valet Spencer and the other servants –as if inspired by a sense of justice – talked as much now of his devotion as they had before of the couple's bitter disputes.

This story – enlivened by details added by Spencer, who possessed more of a fancy for the melodramatic than respect for the truth – spread all over Town and out into the country. Soon it was common knowledge as far away as Scotland, and even went the rounds of polite society in Rome.

Friends and relatives called, and went away again

not only shocked at Sophia's state, but dismayed at Willoughby's appearance. During this period of impeccable behaviour, he now looked positively wild-eyed and haggard, and altogether much as they thought that he should have looked, when he was being dissolute. Then, he had looked bright-eyed and glowing with disgraceful health and hearty spirits. Now, his eyes were as tormented and as hollow as anyone could require; his waist was hollow too, for he had lost weight and had never had much fat.

He never went out in the evenings now. Often, when not in his wife's sickroom, he wandered gloomily about the house, resembling, the servants were agreed, a lost soul. Spencer scared the under housemaid by saying that because of this, his spirit would continue to walk in the house long after he was dead.

His friends urged him to take some diversion. He replied acidly that they knew as well as he did that he had already had too much of that in their company.

At this, Mr. Lequeux felt compelled to speak out: "There is no point in tearing yourself to pieces in this way."

It was a sign of the strength of his feelings for his friend that he actually ventured into the area of emotion. Generally, Mr. Lequeux had a dread of discussing such matters, and would turn aside his own personal misfortunes with a light quip. If anything embarrassed him, it was poetry, especially love poetry, for love was a closed book to him. He had made a marriage of convenience himself, and thought Willoughby's own to the heiress former

Miss Sophia Grey as entirely sensible in a handsome young man then thrown upon the world
without resources.

He regarded Willoughby's passion for Mrs. Brandon as absurd in a sensible man with the right
appreciation of a horse, a dog, a straight left, a fine
hand at cards and a well turned ankle. However, as
Willoughby never spoke of his feelings for Marianne to Lequeux, it was rarely brought to his
notice.

It had been spectacularly, when five years since,
Willoughby had heard of Miss Marianne Dashwood's proposed marriage to Colonel Brandon. At
that time he had raged about it, even threatening to
insult the Colonel and instigate a duel, for: 'I owe
the damned old stick one, anyway'. His friends
had talked him out of this notion and he had settled instead into bitter resignation to the inevitable.

Lequeux was aware that relations between Willoughby and his wife were strained. Still, as this
state of affairs was more or less the case in all his
friends' marriages, it seemed normal to him. Sophia
Willoughby struck him as a scold with a plain face,
so that now he thought that Willoughby was taking concern and remorse to ridiculous extremes.

He realised that one might become attached to
a wife, however disagreeable. He conceded that
he had felt the same way about a horse —always
skittish and inclined to snap —who had also broken her leg. In much the same way, he had also by
degrees, become attached to the wallpaper in his
bedchamber. This he had never thought he liked,
yet he found he was sorry to lose it, when it came
to be damaged by a leak to the ceiling. In fact, he

would rather have passed time in the company of the horse or the wallpaper than with Sophia Willoughby.

However, he did not voice these thoughts to Willoughby. He sensed that his friend might, in his strange mood, take them amiss. Now, he merely concluded his speech with the words, "It is hard. Still, that is life; nothing to be done about it." Having tormented himself by raising such an emotional topic, he cleared his throat.

For some moments, his friend regarded him with a pitying look. He then shook his head. "You are an idiot, Lequeux, though you mean well. I have some advice for you in return, though you won't take it. Do make it up to your wife as soon as you can. Don't leave it too late, as I have."

Lequeux stared: "Make up what to my wife? She has nothing to complain of. Damn it, only the other day I spend the whole afternoon at one of her cursed card parties, with a group of frights; neither a decent face nor a well turned ankle among the lot of them. I assure you I had my work cut out." He added in concern, "You mustn't take it too hard, Willoughby, or the next thing you know, you'll be getting religion; it has happened to better men than you."

Willoughby's lips twitched. It was the first time that Lequeux had seen him smile since his wife's accident, though that smile was bitter enough as he said, "That would scarcely be difficult, though you have no need to fear my turning preacher. I am not made that way."

Lequeux's eyes wandered to Willoughby's hair, which was more disordered even than fashion required; then not knowing what further to say, he went off, still anxious.

Willoughby went out occasionally, and it was on one of these forays that he bumped into Sir John in Bond Street. Willoughby was hurrying to the jewellers to buy his wife a ring which he suddenly remembered she had admired only days before her accident.

Sir John — in common with everybody who saw Willoughby these days — was shocked at his haggard look. "My dear Sir!" was all that he could think of to say, but he wrung his hand.

However, Sir John had not been Mrs. Jennings's son-in-law for so many years without it having some influence over his scanty thoughts, and now one of them was, 'The poor fellow is all cut up now; still, it's an ill wind that blows nobody any good, and all that. As poor Brandon has gone off too, at least when it's all over and they have waited a decent period he can have Marianne at last. That is, if she consents to have such a wicked fellow, for he's gone to hell in a handcart these last few years. Still, he is due to inherit from old Mrs. Smith too, so he should soon be living in clover.'

Willoughby bought the ring, and turned his weary steps homeward. He hadn't taken the carriage or the curricle, as he thought the walk would do him good, though the dirty streets, even in this fashionable part of Town, made a dismal contrast to walking in the country. On his way back, he paused to take luncheon at an inn. Here he was smiled on by the barmaid, and smiled back without properly seeing her.

On his arrival back at the house, he met one of

his wife's physicians in the hallway. He braced himself for the usual dismal forecast – he cared nothing for the prospect of a demand for fees. Then he realized that the man was not now wearing a restrained look, but a self-satisfied one, which was as far as his human warmth extended.

"Sir," he now said, "I think we may have cause for hope."

Willoughby stared, limp with relief. Then he rushed upstairs. He smiled to see Sophia Willoughby sitting up and looking decidedly better. In his absence, she had even had her maid arrange her hair.

Her lips twitched at the corners in response to his, but she controlled them and said, "Well, Sir."

There was an underlying humour in her eyes, besides pleasure in seeing him. He also thought he saw in them also a resolution, not only to live, but to live to see him a respectable man, and dutiful husband for herself. Still, he could only be delighted to see her so much recovered from three hours ago, and he came over to take her hands.

He handed her the box with the ring in it. "How lovely, my dear," she said, leaning back on her pillows, for she was still very weak. "Slip it on, and you may give a vow with it you will keep rather better than those you made when you put on this other."

"You may be sure of that." Gently, he took hold of her hands and slipped on the ring her finger.

CHAPTER NINE

A T ABOUT THIS TIME, SIR John rode over
to Barton Cottage, full of triumph at some
additions to his circle. The Palmers had arrived on
a visit to Barton Park and he wanted Marianne
to make dinner with them her first formal outing
since she had come out of deep mourning.

Remembering how kind to her both Palmers
had been when she had been in mourning of a
different type, Marianne could not refuse.

Sir John went on to boast that he had found
a new dancing partner for the neighbourhood
young ladies today. This was a young naval offi-
cer, a Captain Green, who had taken a house in
the area, and was toying with the notion of living there permanently. Sir John had called on him
that morning, and found him a capital fellow who
loved to socialise, ride, shoot and hunt. Not only
that, but he planned to buy an estate somewhere,
and Sir John hoped it would be in Devonshire.

"He's a fine looking fellow, too, so all the young
ladies will be setting their caps at him – beg pardon, Mrs. Brandon, I recollect you have taken me

to task for using that term."

Marianne had to smile. "Why, Sir, fancy you remembering my strictures all these years. I am quite startled that should have taken note of my seventeen-year-old fancies."

At the dinner, Marianne sat next to Mrs. Palmer, and tried to find suitable replies to such comments as, "Why, you are quite a picture in that mauve gown. My dear, you must give me the pattern, for I declare when next one of my older relatives dies, I shall order one just like it."

Marianne was startled to find Captain Green, who was seated next to one of the acclaimed young beauties of the area, gazing across the table at her in admiration, as he had done when they had been introduced before dinner. He looked as if he would like to speak to her, but kept from so doing through being across the table, could only gaze.

As Sir John had said, he was a good looking man, but Marianne thought that he his face was dull compared to the strong features of the Colonel, or the vivacity of someone else.

After dinner, as the gentlemen came into the drawing room, Sir John came up with Captain Green. "Mrs. Brandon, Green here has been telling us some fine tales. Did you know: the greatest danger when a ship is under fire is not from the shot, but from splinters from the wood? I had never thought of that."

He looked as amazed as if coming across something about which he had never given a thought was unusual for him.

Mrs. Palmer laughed heartily. Marianne made a

more suitable response. Then Captain Green went on to speak about Sussex, where he used to live and where Marianne had spent most of her girlhood, while Charlotte laughed some more.

Sir John had the floor cleared for dancing, and Marianne played while the younger and livelier guests danced. If her thoughts strayed to happier times in this very room, when she had danced with the liveliest man in the room, and then later, with another man who rarely stood up, and did it especially to please her, she turned them back determinedly to the present. She was glad to see that now Captain Green was partner to the Miss Allsopp who had sat next to him at dinner, and completely absorbed in her talk.

"All say that Willoughby acts as a changed man, and has shown himself quite devoted during her illness. Long it may it last, and it is happy that Mrs. Willoughby is getting the better of accident. Sure, it's rare enough for anyone to recover from a broken leg without a halting walk to show for it, for setting the bone straight is so difficult."

Mrs. Jennings' younger daughter greeted this piece of news with her usual merry laugh, while Lady Middleton shuddered. "My dear Ma'am, please spare us!"

Though since the onset of her belief that she was an invalid, she liked to refer to vague symptoms of her own, she was both too genteel and too squeamish to bear happily with her mother's talk of fractured legs.

Mrs. Jennings chattered on, doing her best not to sound disappointed at Mrs. Willoughby's being thoughtless enough to live after all, and so to disappoint her of a match between Marianne and Willoughby.

Though by nature kind hearted, Mrs. Jennings had not taken to Sophia Willoughby on the few occasions that they had met in Town. She thought that if Willoughby was a rake, then his wife was a sourpuss. She had intended the widower Willoughby —who would no doubt be sobered – for Marianne as one of her long time favourites.

Marianne's time in half mourning would be over soon enough, and Mrs. Jennings' old affection for Colonel Brandon was no obstacle to her plans, since she was of a mind that all younger people should be married.

Marianne might persist in being inconsolable over the Colonel. That was no deterrent; what with the money that he had left her, and her own still blooming looks, Mrs. Jennings made no doubt that Willoughby would soon find himself cut out once more, and forced to be jealous of some successful rival all over again.

Mrs. Jennings, as a tireless optimist, suspected that she might have found the very man for Marianne in Captain Green. He admired the lovely young widow; that was obvious. Still, Mrs. Jennings was not sure of him; he might be attracted to one of the younger and livelier local girls.

Now, as Marianne sat with the widow and her daughters in the front drawing room at Barton

Park, Sir John, who had strolled into the room to greet Marianne, said of Mrs. Jennings talk about broken limbs, "It can be a bad business, a broken bone. Many a man's life is ruined by taking a tumble and breaking a leg. Never able to ride to hounds after that, or to shoot game neither…Yes, when I saw Willoughby a couple of weeks' since, he looked so bad I was of a mind to make him a present of one of Young Folly's pups, just to take his mind off his troubles; but he went off before I could speak of it."

He glanced out of the windows, which gave a view over to the paddock, where one of the grooms was giving the younger Middleton children a riding lesson. They shouted as if in competition to make the most noise. Sir John laughed. "Ha! Young Catherine is in fine fettle today. She had better not kick her mount as she does the groom, or she'll be thrown for sure."

Lady Middleton roused herself to fuss about that possibility for the rest of Marianne's visit.

Marianne herself was relieved to hear that Mrs. Willoughby was on the mend. This not because she had the disposition of a saint – being human, it was impossible for her to hear of Willoughby's devotion to his wife without a stab of envy – but because she understood his temperament a little better than her friends.

She saw that had Sophia Willoughby died, in the midst of the ill- feeling between the married couple, Willoughby would have found it difficult to forgive himself all his former neglect of her. The fact that this had been through dwelling on and encouraging his long passion for Marianne, would then prove a great obstacle between Marianne and himself.

Even supposing that the unlucky Mrs. Willoughby had died from her accident, and supposing too, that Marianne had been weak enough to accept Willoughby – his passion for her remaining steady despite that disaster – the thought of their living upon any of his late wife's money was one that must disgust her.

This was leaving aside Marianne's own disapproval of Willoughby's debauched way of life. He might blame it on his unhappy marriage. That was disingenuous; he had lived as a libertine long before, even being unscrupulous enough to seduce Eliza Brandon, then only sixteen. His love for Marianne may have been genuine, but she was not complacent enough to believe –as he hinted – that had he married her, he would have changed his way of life permanently.

No, she felt increasingly that widower or not, she could never have accepted Willoughby. She had blushed at some of Mrs. Jennings's thoughtful looks at her, when news of Mrs Willoughby's danger had first come from town; but this was more because of what she suspected the others were surmising, than on account of her own thoughts.

She was human enough to feel piqued that Willoughby had disregarded her advice, even as he had Elinor's of years ago. Still, she saw that he must come to the truth of these ideas himself. Now she must join Mrs. Jennings in hoping that his change of heart would be permanent.

For all that, she now dreaded meeting with the Willoughbys. Not merely through embarrassment over her last meeting with Willoughby himself, but because she feared her own weakness in allowing her former feelings for him to return.

When the Colonel had been alive, she had felt sheltered from her former love for her fallen idol Willoughby, secured by her own happiness. Now, all that had altered, and with all her disillusionment with his character, the revival of that love seemed to her a horrible possibility. She must do all she could to subdue such a feeling.

This was the more urgent, as in the course of nature, it couldn't be long before Willoughby inherited Allenham. Then, they must meet all too often. This was something she hadn't taken into account when she had decided to move back into Barton Cottage to be company for her mother now that Margaret was to be married.

Now, she diverted the talk by raising an issue concerning the villagers with Sir John.

She was continuing to visit in the village, and to meet with obstruction from Hogg. This was done subtly for so coarse a man. Here, in common with many persons solely occupied in promoting their own interests, Hogg showed himself capable of much shrewdness in pursuit of these aims. Besides, Marianne suspected that he was advised by Mrs. Hogg, who had eased her way through life through flattery and insincerity for nigh on forty years.

Mr. Hogg greeted some of Marianne's minor suggestions for improving the lot of various villagers with a show of enthusiasm. He met the others with tactics of delay, and explained to his master that, "Delicately nurtured female as she was, Mrs. Brandon was too ready to take the locals' word over their hardships, when more often than not, most of their troubles could be traced to laziness and their own negligence."

Sir John was eager to be reassured, disliking the idea that there should be any active suffering in his own village that he could prevent. He rubbed his hands enthusiastically at he told Marianne that, "Hogg was a fine fellow, and she could place all her trust in him."

Marianne placed no trust in Hogg whatever; yet, there seemed little that she could do about his obstruction at the moment.

Elinor and Edward had written back to her advising caution: Hogg was very likely as corrupt as Marianne suspected. Unfortunately, a number of stewards were, especially those with negligent or gullible masters; this probably seemed the worse to Marianne, as both her late father and husband had been such conscientious landlords.

They urged her to make no criticism to Sir John of his steward until she had clear proof of his cor-ruption. Since she had no access to the estate's accounts, that would be hard enough to come by. Realistically, all that Marianne could do, was to try and right the misuse of the funds set aside for the welfare of the villagers in reporting urgent cases of need. Perhaps over time, the discrepancies between her reports and those of Hogg's might rouse even Sir John into querying how his steward managed matters.

Marianne sighed with impatience; still, she saw that this was sensible advice. She went on visiting in the village and trying to make a small difference. The baby with the cough recovered, and without recourse to Mrs. Jennings' Constantia wine; young Harvey continued feckless; and the housewives pursed their lips over his conduct with the women in the area.

Marianne could not help but be struck by the idea that had he been of gentle birth and independent means, he might resemble someone else she knew, who was too often in her thoughts.

"It is very good of you to take over this burden," Lady Middleton sighed from her couch, "It is so tiresome that my health prevents me from exerting myself. The children take up all such energies as I have...I declare young Jack has been halloo-ing down the corridor these last ten minutes: Mrs. Brandon, do pray ring for a servant to send him to shout elsewhere."

Mrs. Dashwood was relieved that Willoughby had removed himself from the area, together with what she called to herself, 'Those insinuating manners of his that might take in sensible persons once, but certainly not more.'

However, she saw nothing to concern her in Marianne's demeanour after his leaving, or of obvious signs of unease when his name came up in conversation during visits to Barton Park.

Mrs. Dashwood still liked to sigh with her daughter over their loss of the Colonel and his virtues – virtues which a neutral observer might have noted increased day by day, until they threatened to become alarming. Marianne, of course, agreed with these panegyrics, but found them painful, and thought that they belonged to an earlier stage of morning. If she was forever to dwell on all that she had lost, she could never look to the future with any equanimity. She must accept that she was no longer the wife of Colonel Brandon, and the mistress of Delaford, but his widow, and once again the tenant of Sir John Middleton.

Fortunately, even Mrs. Dashwood was kept from her wish to wring every ounce of pain that she could from one daughter's early widowhood by another daughter's approaching wedding, and her conflicting joy in this. Margaret was naturally in the highest spirits, and her mother and sister felt that they must do what they could to match them as the wedding day approached.

CHAPTER TEN

"IT'S ALWAYS THE SAME WITH these fellows who get some maggot into their heads about turning virtuous," Captain Shaw said to Mr. Lequeux. "It never does 'em any good, and it never fails to make 'em as miserable as sin. Willoughby does his best to put a bold face on it, but he's got that hang dog look about him of the henpecked man, when he thinks no-one's looking. I call it a shame."

"I call it dammed foolishness," replied Mr. Lequeux succinctly. His own look at he surveyed his hand of cards might have been termed 'hang dog'. "Are you for another bottle?"

"Of course not: send for two. –Now, that serving wench has a nicely shaped ankle; I wonder if she has a calf to match? Do you care to bet on it?"

Willoughby himself shared his old associates' sentiments more than he cared to admit. He still went out with them and their set – "At least you can say that for him," conceded Captain Shaw – but he left them when they started on their habitual excesses.

This gave him many empty hours, despite his

keeping his wife company as much as he could;
this was often a weary task. Not everyone's temperament is improved by ill health, and Sophia
Willoughby continued to be ailing, while her
nature had never been sweet.

She may have risen to the sublime in her talks
with Willoughby on what she thought to be her
deathbed, and now she saw that he strove to please
her and treated her with affection, and she was
gratified by that. Nevertheless, the stings and slights
he had inflicted on her for so many years must ran-
kle, and the insolent air with which he had insisted,
during heated quarrels in the past, how Marianne
was the only woman he had ever loved, must come
back to haunt her.

She brooded, 'He fell for her only because he
found her pretty and sweet natured. As if any
woman wouldn't be good-tempered, with so many
admirers running after her! He never pretended
that he found me to be either. He took me for my
fortune, though he may have come to be as accustomed to me as he is to his oldest pair of hunting
boots.'

She was often short tempered with him, and
above all, demanding; she insisted he accompany
her to all sorts of events he had avoided before.

'And dull work it is. She's punishing me,' thought
Willoughby, as he paced in his dressing room, aiming a kick at a footstall, 'But I fully deserve it, and
worse. I treated her too badly for her to forgive me
easily; but it's still damned hard to bear.'

He was struggling not to think of Marianne. This
had been less difficult, when an anguish of guilt and
anxiety over his wife tormented his every waking

hour and haunted his dreams at night.

Now that she seemed in a fair way to recovering her health – save for the troublesome breathlessness continuing to plague her – he found it increasingly difficult.

Glancing up, he saw that his valet Spencer regarded him with sympathy. Finding this intolerable, he asked curtly for his other coat. Willoughby was to accompany his wife to an assembly. Some of her friends he liked least were to be there, and he was not looking forward to it one iota.

She wore a new dress, a Tambour embroidered creation in palest pink, and he made a point of complimenting her on it. He also stayed by her side through much of the evening. As she did not dance – her leg was not sufficiently recovered for that – he did not dance either, though she urged him when one of her friends looked as if she wished for a partner.

She was well aware of the jealous looks some of the women in the company gave her. Willoughby, now he'd lost that haggard look, was once again among the most handsome of men. He never lost that ease of manner that her city friends' husbands could never acquire. She was proud of him, as of a fine possession.

For all that, her tone was almost querulous as she said, "I saw you look sardonically on Mrs. Jacks earlier, when she spoke of her guests."

Willoughby thought he had behaved with punctilio, and kept his face as blank as a footman's, but something in his look must have given away his thoughts.

"You have a fine nerve to scorn my friends as

vulgar," his wife went on. "What of Lequeux and that awful young man who will take his boots off at the card tables?"

Willoughby grinned, "That's his superstition, and as stupid as such fancies always are. He once made a killing with his boots off, and fools himself that he may regain that luck by continuing to play without them."

He laughed, but broke off as he saw how out of breath she was, and how heavily she leaned on his arm. It came to him how often she was out of breath now.

"You weary," he said. "Does your leg pain you? I'll bring you some wine. We shall have you doing a reel soon enough if we take it slowly."

He spoke cheerfully, and she nodded agreement. But a stir of unease ran through him as he looked at her, and saw how much rouge she had on to give herself the look of natural health. He had told himself that she would soon be as lively as ever. Now he began to doubt it.

Over breakfast the next morning, he asked her if she would like to make a trip to Allenham House. He owed Mrs. Smith a visit. He had not seen her since Sophia's accident.

"I don't know," she eyed him suspiciously. "I suppose you have had another summons from her you feel you must obey. If I go with you, she'll start nagging about us moving into Allenham again. For goodness sake, we have been quite taken in! She's had you at her beck and call these eighteen years, and all the time insisting she's not long for this world, and as like as not she'll outlive us all. It's always the same with these people who've got a fortune to leave."

"She's always eager for a visit; she gets lonely," muttered Willoughby. "I've become used to her, for all her narrow ways, and I'll miss her when she goes."

She eyed him still more narrowly. "I suppose you said much the same of me, when I was in danger?"

"Don't be ridiculous; that was altogether different."

"Is Brandon's widow still in the area?"

He didn't look guilty. "I don't know: very likely not. I wish you would come to Devonshire, or to Somerset. A visit to the country would be just the thing for you."

Sophia Willoughby brooded, and decided that he might be right. She would accompany Willoughby on a trip into Devon, and so keep her eye on him. With any luck Marianne would have left the area.

CHAPTER ELEVEN

M RS. SMITH WAS PLEASED TO see Willoughby, and not displeased to see his
wife. They both noted the changes in each other
brought on by illness, and came to certain conclu-
sions about this that made each disposed to judge
the other more kindly than before.

The Willoughby's visit went smoothly, for Mrs.
Brandon had gone to stay at the vicarage at Delaford in readiness for the confinement of one of her
old friends there.

Lady Middleton told Sophia Willoughby this
when she went over to visit at Barton Park. She put
it as delicately as she could, having a great dislike
for the female love of discussing the most intimate
details of their own and their neighbours' births,
the moment the men were out of the room – her
mother Mrs. Jennings naturally being the greatest
offender.

Lady Middleton saw a less graphical interest in
the effects on the health caused by motherhood
as a different matter. This only applied to those of
genteel birth, of course; rude peasants coped very

well with it. Convinced as she was, that she had become a confirmed invalid since the birth of her youngest, she always welcomed sympathy and offers of help in her household as no more than her due.

Sophia detested unruly children in general and the Middleton children in particular. She had no intention of making any offers with regard to their entertainment. Still, she was prepared to sympathise with Lady Middleton over her health, having much respect for a title, even so minor one as that of baronet.

Lady Middleton roused herself to ring for refreshments. She liked Mrs. Willoughby, in so far as a woman of her narrow sympathies could like anyone out of her own family circle, and sympathised the more with her now as a fellow invalid.

"I trust you do well, Mrs. Willoughby," was her languid query.

"It is kind in Your Ladyship to ask, but I fear not," her guest replied, "I am plagued by palpitations and breathlessness, and my pulse is shocking."

Lady Middleton sat up. Failing to notice that her visitor's whole appearance fitted exactly with such symptoms, unlike her own, she said in a tone almost sprightly, "Indeed, I am sorry to hear it. My own pulse races alarmingly, and…"

Meanwhile, Sir John and Willoughby had ridden into the village. Sir John did not often ride this way, finding the cramped cottages and narrow lane mildly disconcerting. However, he made an exception today, as before leaving Barton, Marianne had advised him that the wall of one of the outermost buildings was in a shocking state of repair. She had said, her face oddly blank, "Mr. Hogg seems to have so much on hand, that he overlooks such matters."

Now he thought that he might as well take Willoughby this way so that he could look it over himself before going on to enjoy a canter through Barton Valley.

"Mrs. Brandon asked me if I'd have one of the cottage walls repaired," Sir John said, as they rode towards Barton Village, passing the odd, cap doffing farm worker.

Willoughby was silent, and seeing his thoughtful look, Sir John remembered their past history again and cleared his throat. They soon came on the cottage in question.

Sir John whistled; the wall was in a miserable state. "I can't think what Hogg was about, letting it go like that."

Willoughby suddenly spoke, "I ought to do more at Combe Magna, though it's a far smaller estate. I leave it too much to my own steward, who is only at the work part of the time and a lazy fellow besides."

"Lazy, that is it!" exclaimed Sir John, in whom the wretched sight of the dwelling with its crazily sloping wall had inspired thought on a topic apart from sports for a whole two minutes. "Hogg says they're a shiftless lot; but it cannot just be that."

"That wall didn't get that way through their leaning up against it, smoking their pipes," remarked his companion.

Sir John, after a startled look at him, burst into a shout of laughter. "To be sure, you are right. I shall tell Hogg to bestir himself about it the next time I see him. He cannot be as hard worked as all that, for he's fat enough. Now, Willoughby, about Young Folly's last litter…"

Willoughby rode home preoccupied. Marianne was wrong in thinking that he had discounted her advice about his treatment of those whose happiness must depend in part on his actions.

It was true that when he first went back to Town, he had angrily dismissed it. During his wife's illness those words had come back to him and had added to his torment, and he had been consumed by yearning to turn back the clock, that he might relive those weeks at least without neglecting his wife.

Now he remembered that Marianne had also mentioned his present and future tenants, and he saw a way to fill his empty hours. He approached Mrs. Smith during dinner on the matter of helping out with the running of the estate at Allenham.

His wife stared to see him speak so far out of character. "We are only here a few days; there scarce seems any point. Besides, you are rather ridiculous in the role of a benefactor."

Mrs. Smith though, was pleased, saying it would be a great relief to her if he could see her steward about it. Willoughby cut short his after dinner interlude with the port to go and see him.

That his only companion today over this was an abstemious neighbour, whose sense of humour could only be discovered through a magnifying glass, probably played its part in this, as much as his continuing unease with his conscience, and the concern that niggled at him about his wife's health.

Willoughby's interview with Mrs. Smith's steward proved less frustrating than Marianne's own with Sir John's man. Mrs. Smith's deputy was honest enough, but as with Willoughby's man on his own estate at Combe Magna, he could devote only a few hours to this role. This man was overwhelmed by various calls on his time, and well aware that there were problems on the estate that had for years been in need of attention. He was relieved to hand over responsibility, if only for a few days. Willoughby resolved to ride out the next morning.

"Quite the industrious squire, Sir? We will see how long this mood lasts," Sophia told him in the drawing room later, while she tinkled at the piano, and Mrs. Smith dozed in her chair.

Mrs. Smith stirred. "No, not at all. I insist that the Duke of York will never succeed to the throne."

"You are no doubt in the right of it, Ma'am," Willoughby returned solemnly. Satisfied, she closed her eyes. He went on, addressing Sophia, "We are not here long, but it's as well to see how things go on; I've been careless enough about it all before, I know."

"Don't be late back for our outing with the Middletons, anyway, as you shall be driving us."

Willoughby would perhaps not have been human if he hadn't remembered another outing with the Middletons years back, where he had impressed another with his skill at the reins, and taken her to see this very house. That had been the time when he had intended any day to do the honourable thing, satisfy his heart, and propose to Marianne.

Now, he recoiled from that memory as if it might sting him —as indeed it did —and he jumped up from his seat. "Shall I give you a song, Sophia?"

Fired with enthusiasm for anything that took his thoughts from the dismal round in which they flowed of late, Willoughby rode over the next day to the home farm.

The farmer was out on business, but his wife was in the kitchen and complained long and loud about the flooding in the cellars. She looked dubious when Willoughby assured her that he would try to have it looked into. Still, she pressed home made wine on him; this he knocked back in one draught, to avoid the taste.

Overwhelmed by his suavity, the woman told anyone who came by over the next few days that the young master, when he came to inherit, would prove a fine landlord. Surely the stories about him could not possibly be true, such a nice way with him as he had.

"We'll see if anything be done about there cellars, for all his fair speeches. You watch out with that sort of gentleman," retorted her husband.

From here, Willoughby rode on the hamlet, which he thought miserable enough. The younger men were all out in the fields. When he knocked on the door of the nearest cottage, the elderly woman he saw through the window, sitting in a chair and surrounded by small children, seemed not to hear him.

A neighbour came through her door – left open for reasons that would soon become apparent to

Willoughby –and hurried to usher him into her own smoky, cramped interior, where he stood with the ceiling only an inch above his head.

In between coughing fits, he promised to see what could be done about the ventilation, and cast horrified looks at the evidence of poverty and cramped living all about him.

Hurrying out into the fresh air, with a hundred good resolutions, he found himself regarded as he stood clearing his throat. He turned to see that a poorly dressed, round-eyed small girl of perhaps three gazed at him. It seemed to him that she resembled the infant he had prevented from plunging into the wall that day with Marianne. Very likely, in this small community, they were related.

This child calmly took his hand – with a trust that Willoughby could not help feeling entirely misplaced – and solemnly led him into her own cottage.

Here, a young woman was cutting up vegetables for soup, while a baby sat clamouring in a box. Willoughby now realised that these might be the family of the man whom the gamekeeper at Sir John's suspected of poaching. Certainly, there was a skinned rabbit on the board and the woman had started at his entrance. Yet after all, rabbits were common enough in the area.

In any case he cared nothing for the anxieties of the gamekeepers as he stood clutching the child's hand and looking about, coughing some more, for the inside of this cottage was also smoky. He only saw their want. He swore to get something done about these damnable fireplaces if it was the last thing he did.

Under the cover of the baby's squalling, he placed some coins surreptitiously in the child's hand. "For Mama," he urged, "Don't eat 'em, eh?"

He left, waving away the woman's flustered apologies for the state of the place, and hurried to his horse to be back in time to ready himself for Sir John's trip to a local beauty spot.

The weather being fair and Sir John's cooks having produced the best of food for the hampers, everyone was in high spirits. Mrs. Willoughby chancing not to be out of temper and a good deal less breathless than of late, the trip was an enjoyable one, even for her. Sir John talked and laughed loudly, and Lady Middleton smiled now and again.

Only the youngest of the girls had less pleasure from the trip than she expected. Miss Amelia had thought, on hearing of Willoughby, that as he was over thirty he must be almost elderly. On seeing him, she changed her ideas, finding him the most handsome man she had yet seen. In fact, she began to doubt there could be another such in society to compensate for his having been already taken.

This cost her a few pangs over her cold chicken and slices of apricot cake. Her older sister, whom she thought wholly sophisticated, having already had one season, looked shocked when Amelia confided in her that a married man so much older had taken her fancy. Still, she was quick to assure her that more handsome men crowded the streets of every big city.

The next morning Willoughby met with the man who generally did the building repairs for Allenham. A disappointed Willoughby had to defer his scheme of dealing with the flooding of the cellars in the home farm as too expensive to be undertaken without Mrs. Smith's consent.

However, with his coughing fits in those cottages still vivid in his mind, he was determined that something must be done to lessen the amount of smoke billowing back from those fires, even if he had to pay for it out of his own pocket. Here, the man had a couple of good ideas about how to mend matters which were inexpensive. Willoughby set these works in hand and went whistling into breakfast.

The hours by the sea seemed to have done Sophia Willoughby good. As she sat at the breakfast table, he fancied she had more colour to her face, and that her breathing was easier.

Despite this, it was one of the days when she was out of humour. He felt almost virtuous in sipping coffee. Before he had drank beer with his breakfast, but stopped as part of his resolve to reduce his alcohol intake. His wife asked him in a tone half teasing, half taunting, "So, Sir, on your mission to do good works yesterday, did you meet with a wide-eyed village maiden?"

"Only one not yet four years old," replied Willoughby, suddenly seized with an urgent concern for that child's future, which he must do something to ensure.

This was one of those times when his own future, as he tried to amend his ways, stretched long and bleak before him. He did his best to be patient with his wife. Since her accident, he had never allowed himself to forget again that if he could never love her as he had adored Marianne, he had become attached to her in another way. He had always known how she adored him, and was determined to treat her as kindly as he could.

He was equally resolved to leave his debauched, careless way of life behind him, let Sophia taunt him all she pleased. Still, the struggle ahead would be a hard one.

He had weakened a little here and there in his resolutions. Sometimes, he had shown his impatience with Sophia, and taken too much wine in an effort not to brood about Marianne; yet always, he had reined himself in, much like a horse.

The simile was an apt one, for the last time he remembered being so resolved about anything had been when, as a small boy, he had made up his mind that he would learn to sit a horse as easily as his then hero, his older cousin.

Still, he found improving his character a wearying effort; Sophia's sour face and carping remarks made it unrewarding besides. If only he could lose his love of Marianne, it would be far easier. He tried to bury those feelings as he had before, when she was married to that detestably worthy Brandon. He did his best not to think of her, but she was constantly at the back of his mind, and appeared in his dreams.

Now, she was a lovely widow, still only in her mid twenties, and looking younger. The time of her mourning was coming to an end. Brandon had ensured she had independent means; it stood to reason that she must have admirers.

He remembered once again how the thoughtless Sir John had said something about this Captain Green's coming to the area, and his admiration for Marianne. Now, Willoughby gritted his teeth and tried to thrust the idea to the back of his mind, as he had done so many times already.

CHAPTER TWELVE

BACK AT DELAFORD PARSONAGE, MARI-
ANNE was delighted to see Elinor and Edward
and her nieces and nephews again. It was bitter
and sweet to see Delaford itself, now the home of
someone else.

Colonel Brandon's young heir was there. Marianne called on him. He looked dismayed to meet
with his relative's relic. He acted as though in ter-
ror that she might break down into lamentations at
any moment.

"Er, how do you do, Ma'am? Very good of you to
call. Er, er…" he looked at a loss for words.

"I have decided to move back to Barton Cottage
in Devonshire," said Marianne.

He had replied hastily, rubbing his hands violently, "Devonshire! I quite envy you, living there,
a lovely county, Ha, Ha!"

Back at Delaford parsonage, Marianne looked
anxiously at herself as she adjusted her hair at mir-
ror in the guest room. Surely she was not quite
such a tragic a figure as he seemed to find her?
She was now wearing the colours of later mourn-

ing, light mauves, lavenders, and greys. These suited her well, bringing out the warm tones in her skin and hair. She was, of course, rising twenty-five, and must seem nearly middle aged to a youth barely eighteen.

Willoughby had been twenty-five when they had first met on the hill near Barton where she had twisted her ankle. He had seemed youthful enough to her, but then he was a man. Women were seen as aging far more quickly. He had been so vigorous, so full of spirits, and when he – but she wouldn't allow herself to think about him.

Elinor seemed to look at her with too much penetration, guessing that that her sister had some source of unease besides her loss of the Colonel.

To divert her, Marianne exerted herself to be lively: "Really, Sir John seems to have more energy than ever; it is quite startling. When not shooting and riding out to hounds, he is still full of a hundred schemes for balls and outings."

"He is to be congratulated," smiled Edward, "But perhaps he is helped in it through being troubled with so little mental activity."

Every day, Marianne visited the friend who had recently been confined. Elinor came with her now and then, but as her own baby was due in a few months, she was often fatigued herself from her own concerns.

Marianne would have been happy to be tired herself, if she could have a family of three and another expected. The sight of her friend's new baby often gave her pangs of regret as she walked the half mile back to the vicarage. She arranged her face into a cheerful look before Elinor saw her, but

Marianne suspected that her sister was not fooled; she seldom was.

"An irreversible decline of some sort," said Mrs. Jennings. "The doctors have given her up, poor creature. I know they did as much last summer, when she had her accident, but from all I hear this trouble precedes this. Poor Willoughby has been all attentiveness, by all accounts, taking her to the sea and for the waters at Bath, though neither of them did her any good."

"Oh dear," Marianne could think of nothing else to say. She could only hope that Mrs. Willoughby's months of ill health had to some extent prepared him for losing her.

"Certainly, they can't fault his treatment of her since she had that accident; that is one good thing. It's a shame, but such is the way of the world. When one person enters it, another leaves it. On that, I see you grow a fine size, Mrs. Ferrars. I am happy to see you again and looking so blooming as you swell. "

Lady Middleton roused herself. "Mama, the wind gets up outside."

"There is nothing wonderful in that, Mary, when there have been gales these last few days. Aha! In weather like this, Captain Green may be thankful he is not at sea, eh?"

Mrs. Jennings now looked thoughtfully at Marianne, who had taken this opportunity to go over to the window to look out at the trees swaying in the wind. A process of thought obvious to Elinor led her to say in a stage whisper, "Sure your sister has been a widow well over eighteen months now?"

"Yes," admitted Elinor, adding – with a hope she knew would be vain – to deter Mrs. Jennings' from certain plans, "She remains very much affected, of course."

Elinor saw that Marianne was getting used to going out into society again. Initially, she had felt the same way about meeting people as she had in London immediately after Willoughby's desertion. She found it a trial, but she saw that it had to be done. She could not be a recluse forever, as their mother, who rarely went out herself, joined Elinor in urging. Now she was even beginning to enjoy these outings a little.

Mrs. Palmer said in a stage whisper, "She looks very well, anyway. Her bloom is quite come back. I was thinking so at your other sister's wedding, and by the by, Mr. Ferrars made so fine an address that day. You know, I am sure Captain Green admires the former Miss Marianne, and I must say I don't wonder. "

"Then so much the worse for him," Elinor could not help retorting. Mrs. Jennings smiled complacently. "We shall see, my dear. As I always say, one shoulder of mutton drives another down. It that goes for the dinner, for sure it must be the same with husbands."

Marianne herself could not help overhearing this discussion. These days she was too tolerant to do more than give a weary sigh.

Yet, now she realised that Captain Green could

be said to be am admirer. His attentions were respectfully muted, as became her recently widowed status, but now that she came to think of it, they were gradually becoming more decided. He always listened to what she said with extra attention, for all that it was so much less lively than the chatter of Miss Allsopp and the other young girls, with whom he was animated enough.

Still, she desired the idea of Captain Green's attentions no more than those of any man; it still felt incongruous. As a wife and then a widow, she had got out of the way of being seen as in the position to have admirers. She now saw that she must accustom herself to the idea.

CHAPTER THIRTEEN

WHEN THE DOCTORS TOLD WILLOUGHBY that his wife would not live long, they came to him as a pair, convinced that he would act as unreasonably as he had at the time of her accident.

To their amazement, he heard them out quietly. He only bit his lip and paused some moments before asking them how long they thought she had, and what might prolong her life.

It was when he heard them again recommend remedies already tried —sea bathing and the waters at Bath — that he knew they had given her up entirely.

With leaden feet he trod up to her rooms. She was lying on her bed, and had let fall the book in her hand. Seeing his face, she said, "Ah; they have told you."

He came over to her and took her hands. Above anything, he was concerned that she would be frightened at the idea of death, but he saw no sign of this in her eyes. He was impressed, as so often before, at her courage. He saw now that she had been making up her mind to face eternity for some time now, while he had deluded himself that there must be yet one more cure that might work.

His old shame came on him in full force. He dropped his face on her hands, but not to shed tears. He was long past such comfort as that.

"Look at me," she said.

He did. He waited for her to say something cutting.

"I got what I wanted in you; I knew your character when we married, so I have had nothing to complain of. You have been as good as you can of late, and I married you and would not have had you any other way, for all my hard words, so you must not torture yourself when I am gone. If that Marianne Brandon will have you, you take her. You deserve to be happy at last."

"No I do not! I've treated you shamefully, Sophia, and a few months' halfway decent behaviour cannot make up for that. Do not even speak of my re-marrying! And that's another thing: it is true, I married you for that damned money, though I hope you finally believe me when I say that things changed, and I came to see I do feel love for you, though it took your accident to make me see it clearly."

Here she smiled, and without irony. "I do know that now." As before, she put up a hand to caress his face.

He bit his lip again and went on unsteadily, "I am glad at least that after your accident I made all your money that came to me on our marriage over to you. Good thing I am skilled at cards, as by then I had spent so much time at the tables I'd have squandered the lot long before otherwise, and never been able to make it over to you again. Mind you leave it to someone else, if you must go before me, Sophia…" He broke off, gazing at her. He saw the hopelessness of any appeal to her on this in everything about her, and bit his lip again.

After a few moments he finished unsteadily, "If you must leave me anything, let it be five or ten pounds, such as you would leave to a servant, and no more. A miserable fortune hunter deserves no better than that: less, if anything."

She spoke with only minimal acidity, "This is foolishness, my dear, and all of a piece with all these whims about helping the poor on the estates. It is too incongruous; you will never make a good man, so you will be serving the world a poor turn if you abandon being at least an amusing one."

"Don't say that, Sophia! If you say so, I might as well give up on myself: you ever forgave my outrages."

Under his look, she was forced to make a retraction. "It is true you have done your best to be as good as you can this while, and to me especially. I always knew you are not half so bad a man as you believe or would have us all believe. –Still, I refuse to leave my money elsewhere. You took me for it, after all, and have had to endure enough from me in return for your own wrongs. It is only fair that you should endure my fortune as well when I have gone."

He almost groaned, "No! I took you as the vulgar fortune hunter you have called me – but tell me again that you see that I care for you."

Now she melted: "I do know that. You have often

made me happy, and not just of late. If I could live the time over, I would still make the same choice. I would be kinder to you, besides: as for my so often calling you a fortune hunter, you were sensible to do as the world advises in making a marriage of convenience."

"Hush, you become breathless." His voice was unsteady again, and it was a long time before he could say any more himself. Then he said, raising his head, "No more talk of the damned money: I wish it at the bottom of the Thames. Tell me instead what I can do for you."

She caressed his face again. "Then, let us go to Bath again. I liked it there."

They did go to Bath. Willoughby did not generally care for the town himself as too quiet. The days were long since gone when gallants with red heeled shoes had strutted through its fine squares and wide streets in pursuit of beauties with high piled powdered wigs, and every kind of excitement could be found there.

Now, that very sedateness matched his current mood, and he would do almost anything to please his wife.

"Willoughby's off to try the waters on his wife one last time," Mr. Lequeux told the Honourable William Ashton − to whom Willoughby had said more than once that it was as well that his title gave him some claim to that description. "Anyone would think it had been one of those love matches, from the way he goes on."

Lequeux cleared his throat at the use of the word 'love'. "He has a bad conscience, poor fellow, that is what it is, and that's deadly." He nodded sagely. His own conscience, regarding his own misdemeanours, was entirely at ease, for the simple reason that he it had atrophied through lack of use.

The Honourable William Ashton shook his head. "Come to think of it, if he had made such a match he would never be so cut up. They always end with the parties on worse terms than if they had started off detesting each other. I was warned off them by an uncle, who had been fool enough to make one himself, though a sensible fellow in every other way. Marrying for love, he said, is like going into a duel with a blindfold; you cannot even see your opponent."

These gentlemen, in their disappointment in losing Willoughby as a boon companion, did not do him justice. He only sometimes looked melancholy, though inwardly he was wretched. He still saw his old friends regularly when he was in Town. Still, he continued to avoid joining them in their excesses, and as he never now played for high stakes, had virtually debarred himself from the Cocoa Tree. He had largely given up drinking brandy, and seemed to feel no temptation to linger outside the Opera House talking to the girls.

When Sophia Willoughby had seemed on the mend, his old friends had teased him about his mending his way of life, and done their best to help him back on the right path. They had no luck in this. Willoughby remained obdurately moderate in his drinking, and couldn't even be laughed into excess.

He told them: "The sight of you in the morning, Lequeux, is enough to make an abstainer out of anyone; and the drivel you chatter to those women of the town, Ashton, is worse than the speeches in the worst play I ever saw."

Leaving them shaking their heads, he travelled swiftly back through the illuminated London streets to see how Sophia did. As the obsequious footman closed the door on him, he stood in the hallway, listening to the heavy tick of the great clock, and wondering if he ought to pay a quick visit to Allenham again.

He was reflecting that these days, his life seemed to consist of sad days divided between two sick-beds, just his valet Spencer appeared. His man had arranged his face in such a sepulchral look that Willoughby knew the news he bore at once.

"Well, it's very sad." Mrs. Jennings told Mr. Palmer. "They say she long had trouble with her heart, and it was that killed her, not the broken leg."

Mr. Palmer showed restraint in not remarking that from his own impression of Mrs. Willoughby, he was surprised to see she had one at all. He thought her a terrible woman, whom Mrs. Jennings normally rightly summed up as a scold and a sourpuss.

His mother-in-law went on, "They all say it was Willoughby's excesses that shortened her days.

Frankly, I don't believe a word of it. He has been
dutiful enough these last months, too. They say he
has buried himself at Combe Magna."

Charlotte Palmer said, "It is heavy news, Ma'am…
On a happier note, what do you make of Captain
Green's flirtations? He has quite the pick of the
young ladies round Barton. Whom d'you think he
will settle on?"

Mrs. Jennings brightened. "It is my belief he waits
for Mrs. Brandon to recover from her mourning."

CHAPTER FOURTEEN

MARIANNE HEARD OF SOPHIA WIL-
LOUGHBY'S death with dismay. She
wondered how Willoughby took it. From the third
hand reports, she gathered, he had taken it badly.

"I invited him to come and stay for the shooting
when last I saw him," said Sir John, "Nothing like
some sports for taking a man out of himself."

He said this much as one who needed taking
out of himself. Certainly, of late he had come to
see himself as a man with weighty concerns on his
own mind.

Certain irregularities in Hogg's financial transac-
tions had become apparent even to Sir John's less
than acute mind. He declared himself astounded as
he called his steward to account.

The man assured him that it was all a mistake.
Still, these errors, in combination with certain
differences between Hogg's reports of the village
and Marianne's —which the blundering knight had
felt obliged to tear himself away from his sporting
activities to investigate – had led him to lose some
of his good opinion of Hogg.

Marianne would have liked to see Willoughby, so that she could say something of comfort to him to take away the sting of her last rebukes. He may have deserved them, but she thought his conscience must be tormenting him enough, without his having the memory of her words to make things worse.

Yet, no doubt she was the last person he wished to see at a time when he was wholly taken up with regrets about his late wife. By an irony, now the positions in which they had been when last they had met were to some extent reversed. Marianne was forced to admit how often she thought of Willoughby, while almost certainly, his thoughts were solely concerned with his dead wife.

Elinor and Edward had gone back to their parsonage at Delaford. All remained quiet about Barton as autumn turned to winter and Christmas came and went. Marianne worked hard to keep her mind occupied and not to brood. She had to forbid herself too many solitary walks.

Sir John and Lady Middleton had taken a house in town for the season, for it was now January, and many of the families were headed for London.

Mrs. Jennings, not at all deterred by the disastrous outcome for Marianne of a former stay in Town – when Marianne had learnt of Willoughby's abandonment – urged Marianne to go up with her.

"Lord, my dear, you will be getting too morbid up here in the country, with everyone gone away. You should be getting out more, now that it is so many months since you lost poor Brandon. You and your mother will gape at each other as dull as two cats on your own."

"You are all kindness, Ma'am, and I thank you for your offer. But I expect my mother would be as dull as one cat without me now that Margaret is married. The two widows can keep one another company."

Mrs. Jennings clicked her tongue, and looked at Marianne speculatively. Captain Green was going to Town too.

He called at Barton Cottage before he set off, He was as pleasant looking and suave as ever. Mrs. Dashwood looked on him approvingly, and even more so as he gave the younger widow a look charged with meaning as he bent over her hand.

"I hope we shall renew our acquaintance when I am back from Town, Mrs. Brandon; I am disappointed that Mrs. Jennings could not persuade you to come."

Marianne went on with her studies, and her visiting in the village. Now that Sir John was away, this meant more dealings with Hogg. At least, now he was more cautious in opposing her suggestions for improvements to the villagers' lot. This was certainly on the advice of his hard eyed wife, who regarded Marianne with a sullen deference whenever they chanced to meet. Marianne sighed, and thought how there were not many such landowners as the late Colonel to be found.

Often, she found herself thinking about what people said of Willoughby, and how he had changed from a careless landowner to a conscientious one. Naturally, she wondered if it had been her words which had at last produced that change in him. Then she rebuked herself for vanity in hoping that.

She thought over how people said that with Mrs. Willoughby's death, he had not gone back to his wild lifestyle, but lived quietly at Combe Magna.

Then, she stopped herself thinking of him at all, and made herself concentrate on making more soup for the old gardener. But while she made that soup, Willoughby was back in her thoughts again.

Marianne seemed to be forever bumping into one of the Hoggs, or coming across the dissolute young Harvey, the village ne'er do well – while the person she now longed to see she invariably missed.

Willoughby had been to stay at Allenham House since the loss of his wife, but Marianne had been away at Delaford, helping after the birth of another baby –this time, Elinor's fourth.

Willoughby had called at Barton Park a couple of times. Here he had met Captain Green, but he had missed Marianne, who arrived back the day he left for Combe Magna. Marianne wondered what they had made of each other; she was ashamed to find herself hoping that Willoughby might hear something of the Captain's growing interest in herself, and be a little jealous, and...

...At this point, she cut herself off, rebuking herself one more for vanity.

She went on with her studies, and her music. The evenings when she read or sewed with her mother seemed very long now they lacked the diversion of Margaret's chatter. Marianne had to acknowledge the truth of Mrs. Jennings's predictions; the two of them were indeed as dull as two cats.

Hoping for some diversion, Marianne read out parts of Mrs. Jennings's letters from town, full   of the latest news, and came on this: –

*'There is no sign of Willoughby; he remains buried at
Combe Magna, while you, my dear, refuse the diversion
of a season away from Barton. I call that sad. Of course,
my dear, Willoughby is now seen entirely as a catch. All
the young ladies will be setting their caps at him when
he does come back to Town, handsome devil as he is, free
once more , and with his late wife's fortune to boot. I
cannot credit the story that came to my ears, that he gave
that fortune back to her, and she willed the lot away to
others. He could not be such a fool as that –'*

"Why, Marianne, have you stopped reading?
Does the widow write something you think too
vulgar for your mother's ears?"

"No, Mama," Marianne said slowly, "But I've just
remembered a letter I must write myself. It is one
that I think I should have written before."

Marianne could no longer restrain herself. All
her old, passionate, headstrong ways came to the
surface again, and her scorn for convention, and
she wrote to Willoughby.

*'You will be startled to receive this from me, but I have
long wished to condole with you on Mrs. Willoughby's
death.*

*I know it is regarded as improper for me to write to
you at all; still, I have not completely lost all my old,
unlucky habit of setting the rigid rules of polite society
aside, whatever idea I may have given you lately to the
contrary. I scarcely need urge you to say nothing of this
letter to anyone, and to burn it as soon as you are able,
after you have read it.*

I know that it would be idle to pretend, now that Mrs. Willoughby is gone, that your relations with her were always harmonious; but I have ever believed you to have become over time sincerely attached to her. I could not fail to hear accounts of your devotion to her in her ill health, and now I feel for you in your loss, the more because of my own recent bereavement.

When last we met, I used harsh words to you, which I beg you to forget. Again, I would be a hypocrite were I now to pretend that your former way of life was a good one. One cannot avoid hearing tales from persons fond of gossip, and so I must tell you that now I rejoice to hear that you can no longer be accused of excesses even by one who must have sounded sadly self-righteous when last we met.

I hope that you will excuse me the strictures I used then with the knowledge that I wished only for your own good, and my own also.

Whatever your future, my dear Mr. Willoughby – and I must call you that – my thoughts are with you more often than you might believe, and also warmer than you might fully credit.'

M B

Posting this letter without Mrs. Dashwood's knowledge was fraught with difficulty for Marianne. She had to invent an excuse to drive over to the nearest village with a post office where she was unknown to the people. As so often before, she was thankful that now, with her own income added to Mrs. Dashwood's, they could run a gig.

As ever, besides, the country roads she jolted through were muddy and rutted. Yet now, the banks were green with the spring, and she was

surrounded by the song of the birds in the high
hedgerows, the snorting of the cattle and the cries
of the lambs in the fields behind. As she breathed
in the soft air, this clandestine errand made Marianne feel once more as tremulous as a young girl.

As she sent off her letter, she was sure that the
post mistress saw her blush, and it was that which
made her smile.

Marianne blushed many times more over the
contents of that letter over the next few days. She
wondered if she had expressed herself too warmly,
often regretted sending it, and dreaded Willoughby's not responding.

She even feared that he might send back a reply
as cold and insolent as the one she had received,
that other time that she had written to him, in
that time which seemed both long ago and close
at once.

Still, that was foolish. It was the then Sophia
Grey who had dictated that hateful letter, and
Marianne had long understood the jealousy that
had prompted her to that. It had taken Marianne
a long while to forgive Willoughby for agreeing
to write what she dictated. Later, she had realised
it was a mood of wild defiance of his own feelings
that had led him to agree to it.

Marianne thought how the Colonel would have
deplored her writing to any man to whom she was
not engaged – unless the recipient had been himself
in the days before their own betrothal – in which
case, he would have excused it readily enough. But
for her to send such a message to Willoughby, and
after his former betrayal of her, would have struck
him speechless. She could not imagine what he

would have said when he had finally regained the powers of speech.

Of course, the late Colonel had every reason to resent his ward's seducer. Still, his dislike of Willoughby had been fired by another factor to which he had never admitted – the natural jealousy of a passionate man for Marianne's first love.

Meanwhile, Mrs. Dashwood was hoping for a letter of another sort from Town; she hoped for a proposal to Marianne from Captain Green. He surely only needed to be away from her daughter and in the company of the insipid Town beauties a short while to realise her worth – unless he were to prove another vulgar fortune hunter.

Mrs. Dashwood had stopped worrying about Willoughby. After all, they had seen no more of him. She had heard of his reform, and sighed over it, "It was needed, poor young man…" Still, she rather thought that after such wrongdoing, and the grief he had once caused Marianne, let alone his wife, he ought to spend the rest of his days in mortification and remorse.

In this, as ever, she tended to believe that others' wishes entirely coincided with her own, and assumed that her daughter felt the same way.

On the third day, Marianne, still hearing nothing, was overwhelmed by a feeling of restlessness and resolved to take a walk. The weather was fine, though there was a chill breeze.

Almost automatically, she struck out towards that farmhouse near the hill, where she and the object of so many of her recent thoughts had rescued that child from the well.

She had urged the mother to have the well covered with a piece of wood. Marianne knew that overworked, harassed farmers' wives were often more careless about the safety of their offspring than they might be, had they as much leisure as Lady Middleton for solicitude about them. Accordingly, she resolved to see if the woman had indeed had the well safely covered. She used anxiety about this as an excuse to walk that particular way today.

As the roofs of Allenham House came into view, Marianne thought again of the isolated Mrs. Smith. She wondered, as she had so often, if it would be forward of her to call on her. She might well be lonely, however reclusive her nature.

She was nearly up to the farmhouse, overlooked by that hill where she had met Willoughby. She glanced up at it, and saw the figure of a man come round from the other side, aiming for the summit. From his walk, she knew at once who it was.

Now, she reddened all over again. She shivered as she stood still, her heart beating fast, waiting for him to turn his head and see her.

The next moment, Willoughby had caught sight of her. He paused for a moment, gazing at her earnestly; then he was running down the hill towards her. As he slowed his pace at the foot, she tried to still her breathing and compose herself.

They gazed on each other as he came up to her. He thought her as lovely as ever, with the breeze whipping up the colour to her cheeks and the sparkle to her eyes, which had further brightened on seeing him, and he looked on her with the same yearning admiration as of old. Then she knew that his feelings for her had not changed after all.

She saw that he was still as handsome as ever, as

upright, as vigorous. She had seen before, how the years of his former debauchery had failed to ruin his looks, but had written their story in the light lines about his mouth and eyes and that reckless look that lurked at the back of those eyes.

Now, those lines seemed altered; they were rather the lines of sorrow, and there was a slight but indefinable melancholy under his old, merry ways.

He smiled as he made his bow. "It would have been a fine thing, had I twisted my own ankle, for I don't think you could have carried me." He grinned with all the old liveliness; but then, perhaps reminded of his late wife's accident, his manner sobered. For all that, there was joy still in his look still as he went on, "I came at once when I had your letter. You cannot imagine my torment of excitement when at last I believed that I might have cause to hope, after those months spent trying to live a better life and being a good landowner, joyless at Combe Magna. Tell me at once: have I any reason to fear Captain Green as a rival?"

She shook her head silently, and eyes lighting up. He rushed on, "I was gathering the courage to call at Barton Cottage, wondering if Mrs. Dashwood would deny me entrance."

Marianne laughed. "I don't think she would go so far." Their eyes met, and she could see that laugh gave him the encouragement he needed.

"So you are not truly disgusted with me? I thought you must be, after my words last time; and that is following on my earlier miserable humiliation of you, and the dissolute life I led after I married Sophia, who deserved better, even as you deserved infinitely better…But I must be a fool to remind you of my old disgusting acts. You have no idea how I regret them. I soon enough had bitter cause to wish unsaid the words I used to you when last we met. You say that your own words to me were harsh. They weren't harsh enough."

She shook her head. "You were wrong to speak so, but…"

Now he had her hands, and she revelled in his touch and his words: "You will not find me too precipitate, if I ask if I may hope? However badly I may have acted, I have this at least to plead in my defence, that I have always loved you. But I realised too late how I should strive to prevent that from poisoning my life, and my wife's."

She met his gaze. "You may be entirely hopeful."

His eyes lit; he seized her hands and kissed them wordlessly.

She shivered in her warm cloak, as she had not before catching sight of him. She went on, "But you must both allow me time to learn to trust you again – forgive me for saying that –and for you to mourn. You are but six months a widower: that is enough for the world, but not, I think, for you."

He kissed her hands again. "You have too much to forgive me. But I will show you how I can be trusted now. Will you believe I am not the same man as that same damnable wretch who betrayed two women for that money, and then went on to live as a worthless rake? I gave all Sophia's fortune back to her before her last illness, and then had her will it all away…"

He broke off, for she smiled too tenderly up at him, and their lips met in a kiss. She had let him kiss her when first he had courted her. She knew that according to society's strictures, she should not. Still, she had enjoyed it as much as he. Now, it felt just the same.

It was a long time before they drew apart to draw breath. Then he said hoarsely, "And after your comfortable life at Delaford, you will consider a man who is as poor as ever I was? I hope you can believe that I have no wish to lay a finger on any monies left you by Brandon, who was far more worthy of you than I can ever be."

She put her hands on his shoulders. "Will you take my advice now?"

A shadow crossed his face. "So long as it is not that we must part."

"I will never urge that again. What I want to say is that you are as wrong now, when you place the whole of the blame for the times of unhappiness with your wife on yourself, as when you were too lenient with yourself. When one is in mourning, one inclines to such a view. I know that too well."

He stood, gazing down at her, and sighed. "But you had nothing to for which to blame yourself, in your relations with Brandon."

"But I did blame myself, for allowing myself for so long to be too dazzled by you to see his worth. It is well that for those years with him, I could put my old love for you aside. At one time I was mistaken enough to convince myself that I never loved the real man Willoughby, but a vision of him I had made in my own mind."

He flinched, and she hastened to draw him close, laughing softly. "I did say that I have seen my mistake…You may have been wicked, Mr. Willoughby, but I must love you, anyway. Now, I can admire

you too, as I see you put your old way of living
behind you."

He drew her still closer, and they kissed until
they were interrupted by a treble voice calling a
greeting.

It was the toddler they had stopped from falling
into the well. Willoughby took Marianne's arm,
and together they went towards the well to make
sure that it had been covered.

Meanwhile, Marianne thought again of her
secret regarding that well. How she, as a seventeen-year-old in the midst of her passion for
Willoughby, had once on one of her lonely rambles after he had left her to go to Town, tossed
a coin into it. She had then made the wish that
though they might be parted, it should never be
permanent.

After this visit, he said, gazing down on her,
"There is something you must let me do again."

"Another kiss?"

He kissed her again, but when they came apart,
he smiled and shook his head. "I could not resist
that, though I meant to ask if I might carry you
home again? It will be as if we relive the past again."

She laughed. "Whatever will Mama think?"

"I will let you down at the gate."

"And will it not be too much of a strain for a man
of above thirty, when I have gained some flesh?"

Laughing, he took her up as effortlessly as he had
twice before. "You feel no heavier. Your figure is
just as perfect as before, just a little fuller."

That, she thought, was largely because she had
been childless in her marriage to the Colonel.
Now, she had two odd sensations; one was that

the Colonel now, if he could not entirely approve of her second match, anyway did not condemn it outright. The other that was when she married Willoughby, she would not remain childless for long.

EPILOGUE

THE READER WILL NOT BE surprised to learn that Marianne and Willoughby were soon married, but may be startled to hear that Willoughby was true to his word, and went on trying to be as good a man as he could –which as he said, could never be as excellent aone as Colonel Brandon.

As he had also said, he had given away the fortune he had married to gain. He even gave away the couple of thousand pounds that his wife had insisted on leaving to him, spending it on works for his present tenants at Combe Magna and his future ones at Allenham. A fair portion of it went to the family in the hamlet of Allenham whose the child had adopted him that day.

Of course, this extraordinary conduct convinced many of his friends, especially Mr. Lequeux, that he had become a little mad. "To put up with that vixen for years, and then to throw away the money that was his due! The poor fellow is plain touched," he insisted.

But the Honourable William Ashton took

another view of the matter. He said judiciously, "Very likely he is, but that Brandon widow is still a little peach, and he has got her at last, so I cannot pity him."

But if Willoughby was insane, he showed no sign of it in his future life with Marianne.

Willoughby refused also to benefit by the settlement Colonel Brandon had left to Marianne, and so, until he came to inherit from Mrs. Smith, their income was restricted. Still, as he had largely abandoned most of his extravagant ways (though he always retained his love for his curricle) this was less of a hardship for the pair than might be imagined, particularly as after their marriage, they moved in with her.

Mrs. Smith spent her last years at last contented with the Willoughbys, and she adored his second wife as much as she had disliked his first.

Willoughby was only clearly in his cups on six occasions after his marriage to Marianne: – at the births of their children. So moderate was his lifestyle, that his valet Spencer became bored by the lack of drama and entertainment that his master gave him, and took to writing gothic novels of the sensationalist type.

Mrs. Dashwood, Elinor and Edward were at first appalled at Marianne's marrying Willoughby. Mrs. Dashwood had only partially forgiven him for his former treatment of Marianne, for her anger with him had been proportionate to her previous affection. Edward and Elinor dreaded hearing in due course that he had gone back to his old ways, but as time passed, they had to admit that the only members of the family who fully believed in the change in him –Marianne and Margaret –were right after all.

As Marianne could not spend the money left to her by the Colonel on her own family, she used it in part to provide a good start for her nieces and nephews, partly on making life comfortable for Mrs. Dashwood, in part on a bequest to Eliza, and partly on improvements for the tenants at Combe Magna and Allenham.

Mrs. Jennings was delighted that Willoughby and Marianne had finally come together, and she insisted many times over, that it was of her own doing, though how she believed these machinations had been effected, was anybody's guess.

Lady Middleton said that it was odd, and then passed on to complain of a tingling in her left elbow. Sir John said, "Good Lord!" but then went on to suggest that such a fine shot and horseman as Willoughby deserved his luck.

Over the next couple of years, as the impressionable Sir John saw his neighbour and sporting companion doing so much for his tenants, he decided he wished to do more for his own. This lead to such unease for Mr. Hogg, that he shortly afterwards left his post as steward and took over an inn in the vicinity, where he quarrelled regularly with the ne'er- do- well Tom Harvey.

Captain Green was so put out on hearing of Marianne's acceptance of Willoughby that he went to his own room and swore heartily for ten minutes. Still, as he was by nature sanguine, and not given to strong attachments, he soon transferred his affections to Miss Allsopp and married her instead.

Perhaps it is worth adding here that Miss Steele

delighted Mrs. Jennings but making a match with a man of fashion to whom she had introduced her. He was considerably younger than she and had, if anything, less sense. He got on particularly well with Robert Ferrars.

Marianne was sorry that she could no longer visit Eliza and her family, but her own with Willoughby rather more than replaced that loss.

It was often remarked, that after her union with Willoughby, Marianne's complexion, always lovely, became even more glowing, most especially on rising. Many women asked her what her secret might be. As she always blushed on being asked, they assumed she secretly used rouge.

THE END

Printed in Dunstable, United Kingdom

67208307R00077